EXIT 13

THE WHISPERING PINES

JAMES PRELLER

Scholastic Inc.

© 2022 Scholastic Inc.

This book is a work of fiction. Names, characters, places, and incidents are either the product of the author's imagination or are used fictitiously, and any resemblance to actual persons, living or dead, business establishments, events, or locales is entirely coincidental.

ISBN 978-1-338-81044-8

10 9 8 7 6 5 4 3 2 1   22 23 24 25 26

Printed in the U.S.A.   37

First edition 2022

Book design by Katie Fitch

This book is for two fearless readers,
Grace and Ella, my nieces in the West.

—JP

ONE

ASH STARED OUT the side window. They'd been driving since forever. He was in a land somewhere between wakefulness and sleep, reality and dream. The past hundred miles were a groggy, boring blur. The highway was fully dark, not another headlight on the road. The sky seemed starless, blank. The upper atmosphere obscured by clouds.

And, weirdly, the car was moving slowly. Crawling, really.

Willow's voice broke the quiet. "It's so foggy. Can you even see, Dad?" she asked from the back seat. Willow was Ash's older sister by eighteen months, seated an arm's reach away. It lately felt to him that the distance between them was far greater than that.

"Ha, *seeing*—that's overrated!" joked Mr. McGinn. No one laughed. He drove with his neck strained forward, hands tightly gripping the steering wheel. The fog creeped along the roadway like a living thing—twisting, snaking, reaching out with cold fingers. The McGinns were driving through thick clouds, scarcely able to see the road.

"This fog came out of nowhere," Mrs. McGinn said. She sat in the front passenger seat, flicking through her phone. She turned to her husband. "I'm frustrated. There's not a hotel within fifty miles that accepts pets."

Ash, eleven years old, instinctively felt for Daisy, curled up between Willow and himself. Daisy was a goldendoodle, a snuggly, softhearted pet that had grown up with the children.

"Maybe we should pull over," Ash suggested. "Daisy might have to pee."

Mrs. McGinn nodded to her husband.

Without another word, Mr. McGinn eased the car

to the side of the dark highway. "We'll wait out the fog and stretch our legs. And kids—stay out of the road." He pushed a button and the emergency lights flashed on, in case another motorist came zooming past.

"Here? Seriously?" Willow said. "We're stopping in the middle of nowhere?"

"We're somewhere, Will. We just don't know where that is, exactly," Mr. McGinn replied. "Everywhere is somewhere! Isn't that right, kids?"

Willow gave him the dead eye. She looked to her right, past Daisy and Ash and into the murky distance outside the window. She could make out a line of trees not far from the road. It was hard to tell in the dark. "In movies, this is where the ax murderer usually pops out of the forest and chops everybody to pieces. Don't you think, Ash?"

"Willow, don't tease your brother," Mrs. McGinn said. "Besides, they actually don't use axes anymore. Nowadays, it's usually a machete."

Ash clicked the leash onto Daisy's collar. "Ha, ha, so funny." He groaned. "You guys don't scare me."

"Sure," Willow said doubtfully. "Be safe out there, Little Brother."

The family exited the vehicle, except for Willow. She sat, arms crossed, announcing her disapproval. Mr. McGinn sagged against the front quarter panel of the car. His curly red-blond hair and freckled skin betrayed a Scottish ancestry (he could perfectly imitate Shrek's thick burr). Some might describe him as a "big teddy bear" and not be far from the truth. Doughy, soft, large, gentle. Mr. McGinn rubbed his tired eyes.

Absently, Tricia McGinn—tall, with light-brown-colored skin and dark hair that flowed past her shoulders in a shiny wave—squeezed the back of her husband's neck. "You look tired. We could all use a break. Driving in this weather is stressful for everyone."

She returned her attention to the phone. "Signal's gone. That's weird. Suddenly I'm not getting anything."

She looked into the night sky, as if an answer would be provided there. A radio tower, a flickering satellite, something. But the night sky was strangely still. No lights, no stars, no *thing* at all.

As if they had driven into a void.

Ash led Daisy into the grass, tugging gently.

The ground was damp with dew. The fog swirled and circled around them, brushing against Ash's legs like a hungry cat. A cold breeze stirred. A shiver zippered up Ash's spine. He regretted leaving his hoodie in the car. He walked away from the road and the parked car, toward the tree line. The leash went taut behind him. "Come on, Daisy." He pulled. "What's the matter? Are you afraid of the dark?"

The dog's legs remained locked in place. Daisy stared into the trees, unwilling to take another step.

Leaves rustled—a twig snapped.

A shadow moved amid the shadows.

Ash heard a faint thumping, then a rhythmic pounding. He turned to see Willow, knocking at the window to get his attention. She was pointing and saying something. He could see her lips moving.

"What? I can't hear you!" he shouted.

Willow pounded harder, both palms against the pane.

"The trees!" she cried. "Behind you!"

"What? The trees?" Ash called back.

Daisy stared into the dark. She let out a low, rolling growl.

Willow opened the door a crack so she could be heard. She screamed, "BEHIND YOU, ASH! FROM THE WOODS! IT'S COMING!"

TWO

"IT'S COMING!" WILLOW screamed.

Ash felt a surge of fear ripple through his chest. He turned his head to peer behind him. The trees stood like mute soldiers, guarding the secrets of the forest. Something moved, crouched low. And then Ash saw it—two red eyes floating in the dark. Red eyes staring directly at him.

In a panic, Ash yanked the leash and scrambled to the car. He reached for the door handle. *Thunk.* The lock clicked into place. "Let me in, Willow. Hurry up, let me in!"

Willow answered with laughter.

Slow, soft laughter that built to a roar. "Ha, ha, ha!" she cackled, bending over in amusement.

Tricked, pranked, teased again.

Ash looked back. The red eyes had vanished into the woods—if they were ever there in the first place. His parents looked at him with clearly concerned expressions.

"Everything all right, buddy?" Mr. McGinn asked.

"Yeah, yeah, everything's great," Ash answered miserably. Must have been his mind playing tricks on him again. An old habit. His mother said he'd grow out of it someday, but someday never came. He suffered from an imagination that conjured fresh terrors around every corner. Invisible monsters, unseen dangers. What else could Ash do but turn and bravely face them?

The door unlocked. Willow opened it and snorted. "I'm sorry, Ash—but you should have seen your face. Priceless."

Ash glowered. He pulled the door open and barked, "Daisy, inside."

The dog leaped into the car, gladly.

Ash slammed the door shut while remaining outside the car with his parents. He brought his hands to his hair as if to tear it out. "I can't stand her!"

"Hey, now, buddy," Mr. McGinn began. "That's no way to—"

"Leave him be," Mrs. McGinn said. "Willow can be a pain sometimes."

"Sometimes?" Ash said.

"Okay, got me." His mother grinned. "How about 'a lot of times'? Is that more accurate?"

"Hey! I heard that!" Willow grumbled from inside the car, amused.

Ash nodded, grateful, at least, that his mother seemed to understand.

At that moment, a large roadside advertisement flickered awake. Just fifty feet in front of them, lit by bright floodlights, the tall billboard read:

EXIT 13 MOTEL

"STOP BY FOR SOME SHUT-EYE!"

TAKE THE NEXT RIGHT IN 1.5 MILES.

ALL PETS WELCOME!

"Whoa, that's weird!" Ash exclaimed. He shielded his eyes from the glare of the lights.

They stood side by side, staring up at the suddenly illuminated sign.

His mother's phone dinged. She looked down at its white glow. "Wi-Fi's back."

Mr. McGinn shrugged good-naturedly. "Must be the fog. Look, honey. It seems to be lifting."

It was true. The fog seemed to be retreating. Mrs. McGinn gestured to the sign. "What do you say, hon? Seems like a good time to stop."

Mr. McGinn clapped his hands together. "Let's do this!"

They climbed back into the car. It was still night, of course, but the fog was gone and the road was now visible in the headlights.

"I hope they have an indoor swimming pool," Ash said.

"And a vending machine," Willow added. "I could really use some candy right about now."

The car joined the highway and accelerated. The family's spirits had lifted like the fog.

"That was lucky," Mrs. McGinn said. "The sign just suddenly lit up for us."

As the car hurtled toward its destination, Willow turned to look out the rear window. She saw the billboard fade into the distance—and just as suddenly, the lights went out again.

"So strange," Willow said. "The lights—"

"Mom!" Ash complained. "She's starting again."

"Willow, give it a rest, okay?" Mrs. McGinn said.

Willow frowned at Ash. He grinned in return. Ash wasn't proud about tattling; it made him feel babyish. But sometimes he had to go with what worked.

"Hey, let's sing," Mr. McGinn said. "*One hundred bottles of pop on the wall . . .*"

Willow slid the headphones over her ears and turned up the music, loud. She kept thinking about how strange that was—the way the lights flickered on for a few minutes only to die again as they pulled away. *Creepy*, she decided.

Definitely creepy.

THREE

"IT'S A DUMP," Mr. McGinn said.

They had pulled into the parking lot for Exit 13 Motel. The motel was a long, low one-story building with a front office at one end. The curtains were drawn, and one lone green light shone above the entrance. A few cars were parked in the lot, but otherwise the place looked abandoned.

And more than a little run-down.

For Ash and Willow, all hopes for an indoor pool were instantly dashed. This wasn't going to be that kind of place. The four of them sat in the car, deciding what to do.

"It's just for one night," Mrs. McGinn finally said. "We're all tired—and it does take pets."

"Are you sure about this, honey?" her husband asked.

Mrs. McGinn ran a hand across her black hair. She yawned. It was answer enough. She was sure.

The lobby was small and dimly lit. Beige carpeting on the floor and brown paneling on the walls. No one was at the front desk. The wall clock read nine-fifteen. But it felt like it was past midnight. Not a soul stirred.

"Um, hello?" Mr. McGinn called, softly at first. Then again, louder, "HEL—"

A door behind the desk opened, and a tall, thin teenage boy entered. He appeared to be about Willow's age, perhaps a year older. The boy's hair was black and short. His face was sharp and narrow and not unpleasant, with a pinched nose and pale skin. He wore baggy corduroys and a loose, rumpled sweater. "I'm sorry, we live in the back," the boy explained. "I was bringing tea to my mother."

"Yes, hi, we saw the sign on the highway and—"

Mr. McGinn gestured with his thumb toward the window.

"Name?"

The boy drifted to the computer. He gazed at the late arrivals and waited for a reply.

"McGinn. We were wondering if—"

"Yes, McGinn. We were expecting you," the boy said, tapping on the keyboard. He wore a large silver ring on his right thumb. A figure, perhaps a wolf, was etched into it. He read the screen, "Two adults, two children . . . and a pet."

"But we didn't reserve— I don't see how you—" Mr. McGinn said.

The boy looked up without an expression. "Has there been a mistake?"

Mrs. McGinn spoke up. "Two adjoining rooms, please, if that's possible."

"Already prepared," the motel clerk said.

The McGinns exchanged puzzled glances.

"I'm telling you, our phones are spying on us," Willow commented. "They know our thoughts."

No one disagreed.

The clerk wrote the room numbers on a slip of

paper, tucked plastic room key cards in an envelope, and said, "Ice and vending machines are around the corner. You'll find the code for Wi-Fi on a slip of paper in your room. There's an outdoor pool, but I'm afraid it's not heated . . . on account of there's no water." The boy's eyes twinkled at that. He might have found it amusing. He turned to Ash and Willow. "And where's your pet?"

"In the car," Willow said.

"Daisy," Ash said.

The clerk blinked and gave a nod. "We love animals here at Exit 13." He said it flatly, without the faintest trace of emotion. His eyes indicated a ceramic bowl of dog treats on the counter. "Please help yourself."

"Thanks," Willow answered. "I'm starving." She pocketed three treats.

The pale clerk gave an appreciative nod. He got the joke. "Anything else?"

"Um, no, we'll just get our bags and—say, what's your name, anyway?" Mr. McGinn asked.

"Kristoff," the boy replied.

He had a way of standing perfectly still. A bulky

sweater drooped down over his narrow shoulders.

"You seem awfully young," Mr. McGinn ventured.

"It's not so awful," Kristoff deadpanned. He added with a smirk, "Believe me, I'm older than I look."

A sound came from the back room. Nails clicking on a wooden floor. A snarl. And a sudden, muffled thud. Kristoff's eyes shot to the back door, which was slightly ajar. He pushed it shut. "My apologies," he said. "I'll leave you to get settled if there's nothing else?"

There was nothing else.

The McGinns carried their bags to rooms 15 and 16, the last two doors at the end of the building.

Mrs. McGinn passed the key before the scanner and pushed the door open. She sniffed, as if deciding whether to enter. "Oh dear. It's musty."

"At least it's not the Hotel California," Mr. McGinn quipped. "You can check in, but you can't check out!"

His children stared at him, blankly.

It was so typical. Their father was like a Labrador

puppy—enthusiastic about everything, all the time. He explained, "The Eagles? Classic rock? It's a song, 'Hotel California.'" He began to sing and strum air guitar, rather badly, "*On a dark desert highway—*"

"Sorry, Dad," Willow interrupted. "We're not really up on the golden oldies."

"Anyway, it's just one night," Mrs. McGinn said reassuringly. "How bad can it be?"

"I guess we'll find out," Willow muttered.

They carried the bags into their attached rooms.

FOUR

grrrrrrrr

HEY, IT'S OKAY, DAISY. IT'S JUST A SMELLY OLD MOTEL, THAT'S ALL.

ARGGGH! KEEP IT DOWN!

SHHHHH, SHHHHHH.

grrrrrrr

WILLOW! COME QUICK!

THIS BETTER BE GOOD, ASH.

SOMETHING'S OUT THERE. LIKE A BIG ANIMAL. I SAW TWO BIG, RED EYES STARING RIGHT BACK AT ME.

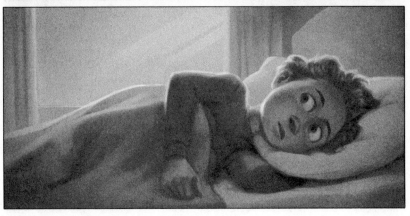

22

FIVE

ASH COULDN'T GET back to sleep. He lay in bed, thinking, tossing, turning. Flipping his pillow over again and again, trying to find the cool side.

There was something he didn't tell Willow.

Words he was afraid to speak.

He lay on his back. The room was lit with a ruby-red glow. He had taken a lamp and placed it on the floor with a red T-shirt draped over it. *Would that cause a fire?* Ash didn't know, didn't care. No way was he going to sleep in the pitch black.

He dwelled on the feeling he didn't share with Willow. It crawled inside him like a snake. Cold and clammy, it coiled around his heart. Ash had felt fear, but there was something more.

Something worse.

And harder to explain.

He had felt . . . *an invitation*.

The creature with red eyes, whatever it was, had been calling to Ash.

Come, follow.

An invitation to enter the woods.

And Ash knew, deep in his heart, that if he had the chance, he would follow.

"Hey, LB?" Willow called in a soft voice. It was Willow's nickname for Ash, *Little Brother*, whittled down to initials.

"Yeah?" Barely a grunt.

"You okay?"

Ash shrugged invisibly in the dark. He didn't answer. He didn't want to say it out loud. No, he wasn't okay. He was scared and confused. Instead, he patted the side of the mattress and invited Daisy up onto the bed.

"Ash, Mom said no," Willow countered. "Daisy has to sleep on the floor, remember? Motel rules. We'll get in trouble."

Ash folded an arm around his big, soft, curly-haired dog. What he needed now was the simplicity and warmth of a dog's love. And Daisy was happy to give it. Ash wasn't in the mood to follow stupid rules.

"Well, in that case," Willow said.

She climbed out of bed and joined her brother and Daisy in bed, the three of them squeezed in together.

"Sweet dog," Willow murmured softly. "Sweet, sweet dog." And after a pause, "Are you sure you're going to be okay, LB? You can talk to me if you want. Nothing happened, right? Just your imagination."

This was something new.

Willow was concerned about him.

Ash yawned, turned to his back, and reached for the tips of his sister's hair. "Mmmm," he said, and fell, at last, fast asleep.

He dreamed of Red Eyes . . . and of following a

path that led deeper into the darkness . . . trees swaying, branches reaching, leaves murmuring . . . and a gathering of shadowy figures in the distance.

Ash awoke to the sound of screams.

SIX

A HIGH-PITCHED ALARM blasted in the room—harsh, piercing, very loud.

Ash and Willow sat up, groggy.

The shrill noise blared, making it impossible to think straight.

The door connecting to their parents' room burst open. *Thump.* The door crashed into the dresser, shivered, and bounced back, *sploinnng*, banging into Mr. McGinn's forehead. He stood for an instant, stunned, then stepped into the room, wild-eyed—*alarmed.* He wore a T-shirt and bright pink boxers.

"Get up, get up, kids!" he cried.

He rushed to Willow's bed and flung aside the blankets. He frantically patted the mattress with his hands. No one there. She was gone!

"Dad, Dad. We're right here," Willow called above the noise.

He spun around in the dimly lit room and, *oof*, slammed his big toe against the bedpost. He hopped in pain on one leg, holding his injured foot in his hands.

"Dad? What's going on?" Ash asked.

The alarm continued to blare at painful decibels.

Daisy leaped off the bed and began barking.

Mr. McGinn, hopping unsteadily on one foot, struggled to keep his balance. He leaned to one side, slumped awkwardly into the wall, and toppled to the floor. "Whoops, *ack, no, neck, oomph!*" he muttered.

Daisy barked at the alarm, at Mr. McGinn on the floor, at anything at all.

BarkbarkbarkyBARKbarkBARK!

It was worse than the alarm.

Mrs. McGinn appeared in the doorway. Green moisturizing cream was slathered all over her face. She glanced around the room, fingertips touching the side of her head. "Fire alarm," she explained in a calm voice. She looked down at her husband on the floor. "I see that your father has things under control."

Ash pulled the red shirt off the lamp, which he brought up to the bedside table.

THUMP, THUMP, THUMP!

Someone banged on the outside door. "FIRE ALARM! EVERYBODY OUT!"

"Mom?" Willow asked.

Mrs. McGinn tightened the belt to her bathrobe. "I don't smell smoke. But we need to step outside, now. Quick, grab something warm, stay calm, and let's go. Hopefully it's nothing."

"Ooooooh," Mr. McGinn moaned, sitting up. "I think I hurt my neck."

"Come on, I'll help you up, my gallant hero." With a warm smile, Mrs. McGinn pulled her husband to his feet. He winced when he put weight on his injured big toe. He held his head in a slightly twisted position, cocked to the side, like a dog that didn't understand what was being said.

The four of them, along with Daisy, stepped out

into the cool night air. In the parking lot, they saw that two other rooms had been occupied. Those people—a couple with three children and a bearded man with a prodigious belly—stood in bare feet and pajamas, looking around in confusion. Daisy appeared to be the only pet in the place.

A fire engine rolled into the lot, lights flashing. The firefighters climbed out of the truck, dressed in protective gear and helmets. The motel clerk, Kristoff, who had checked in the McGinns, stepped out to speak to the firefighters. After a moment, the firefighters seemed to relax. A short firefighter gestured for two others to join her inside the office. She spoke into a radio unit. Minutes later, the alarm stopped sounding.

Kristoff, dressed in black lace-up boots and a dark trench coat, walked along the length of the hotel, stopping to speak briefly with each guest. They scratched their heads, yawned, headed back inside. At last, Kristoff came to the McGinns. He paused for the briefest of moments as he observed Mr. McGinn's blazing pink boxers, knobby knees, pale shins. He glanced at Mrs. McGinn, her face covered in a mask of green moisturizer. Something flickered in his eyes. A private joke. "I'm awfully sorry," he finally said. "There was a small kitchen fire—nothing, really—it's embarrassing—and, well, there are safety protocols to follow. It's safe to go inside. I'm so sorry for your inconvenience."

Mr. and Mrs. McGinn were too tired to talk. Feet dragging, they shuffled into their room. Ash paused at the doorway with Willow. He watched as Kristoff rounded the corner, headed toward the back of the building. Ash shuddered and felt cold all over.

"That's him," he whispered to Willow.

"What? The clerk?"

"Yeah, I've seen him before."

"Well, duh, yeah, he's the cutie who checked us in," Willow said.

Ash frowned at his sister. "Cutie? Him? He looks like a vampire!"

"Yeah, and that's my type!" Willow protested. "The haunted, hunted kind."

"You don't have a type. You never even had a boyfriend," Ash said.

"Did, too. Angel Villar, we had two beautiful weeks together."

"That was third grade!"

"So?"

"So?! You broke up with him when he put jelly in your hair during a spelling quiz."

Willow grinned and held up her hands. "What can I say? We were wild and crazy kids."

"You used to complain that he farted all the time," Ash recalled.

"Well, yeah, there was that—the whole toxic gas problem." Willow paused, thinking it over. "Maybe Angel was lactose intolerant?"

Ash shook his head. He grabbed Willow by the sleeve and pulled her inside the room. "Anyway, *he was the guy* I saw outside the window."

"Angel? My farting boyfriend? What's he doing here?"

Ash groaned.

"I'm kidding!" Willow said. "Lighten up, LB. What do you mean, 'He was the guy'?"

Ash turned serious. "I recognized the way Kristoff walked, like he's leaning into the wind. And the coat, the way it billowed behind him. He was *with* that creature with red eyes. I saw those two go into the woods together."

"You didn't tell me there was a guy," Willow countered.

"I'm telling you now," Ash replied.

"There was a guy and a creature with red eyes?"

"Yes! And the guy was Kristoff!" Ash said.

Willow eyed her brother thoughtfully. *Was he just imagining things? Why didn't he mention it before?* "Okay, color me curious," Willow said. "Let's do it."

"Do what?" Ash asked.

"Let's follow my vampire hottie."

SEVEN

THE SUN AT this hour had not quite cracked the horizon. But the predawn sky was lightening, less than full dark. Somewhere a rooster was thinking about getting out of bed and crowing about it.

Ash and Willow threw on some clothes. They stepped outside and gently pulled the room door shut. It clicked softly. They paused, making sure no one in their parents' room stirred. Around the corner, they reached the ice and vending machines on the side of the building. There was no sign of Kristoff. Willow paused. She reached into her pocket and fished out some coins. "Sorry," she explained, "but I brake for Twizzlers."

Chink-chink-ca-chunk, the coins dropped in. Willow pressed the buttons, B-6. Nothing happened. She pressed them again. Nothing happened all over again. "Stupid machine ate my money," she muttered.

Willow shook the machine, rocking it back and forth.

Hammered at it with her fist.

"Shhh. Forget it, Will," Ash said.

Willow glared at the machine like a sworn enemy.

The back side of the motel had a couple of dumpsters and a large, fenced-in heating unit. A strip of grass rolled gently down into a thick, imposing underbrush. A mass of tall pines towered above. Ash counted the windows of the building and pointed. "I think that's our bathroom." He stood beneath it and studied the forest from that perspective.

Willow did a full turn, 360 degrees. "So where did Kristoff go?" Willow asked, palms raised. "I mean, he came back here . . . and disappeared?"

Ash didn't answer. He walked toward the tangle of growth, bending low, peering inside. "There's got to be an opening. I saw them enter around here from the window."

"The vampire boy and the werewolf?" Willow cracked.

Ash turned to her. "I'm not joking, Will. I saw what I saw—and it wasn't a werewolf. It was like a really big dog, with sharp ears and a long, pointed snout."

"Maybe we should get Daisy for protection?"

"Yeah, funny. That *thing* could eat Daisy for a snack," Ash replied. Something caught his eye on the ground. It was a paw print. A heel and four toe pads with long claw marks coming off each one. Ash placed his hand beside the print for comparison. "It's huge," he murmured.

"Here, let me." Willow snapped a close-up photo with her phone. She adjusted the flash and took other shots of the woods.

"Looks like it went in here," Ash said, ducking down and peering into the tangle of branches, twigs, duff, and leaves. He pushed aside a branch. "Hold this," he said to Willow. "I'm going to crawl through. It might get easier when I get past this thicket."

He began to crawl slowly, cautiously forward. The branches formed a tight tunnel. It looked to Ash like things opened up to where he could stand not too far ahead.

"Shhh," Willow hushed. "Hear that?"

Ash froze, straining his ears. He looked back at his sister, then shrugged.

"The birds," Willow said. "They've stopped chirping."

She was right.

There wasn't a single sound. Not a squirrel chittering or a bird calling from the trees. Even the wind held still. They heard something moving in the distance. Muffled sounds. Crackling underbrush, broken branches, footsteps. Willow reached for Ash's ankle and squeezed. The sounds got louder, nearer. Not walking . . . but running, scrambling. They could hear panting. Something, or somebody, breathing heavily.

Frantic, frightened.

And running hard.

In their direction.

Willow pulled Ash back. "Faster," she hissed. They

both scrambled, crabwalking, tumbling out of the underbrush. They fell onto the mowed lawn and waited, eyes wide, hearts jackhammering. Willow clutched at Ash's shoulder, pulling him nearer. The footsteps slowed, drew closer.

A bloody hand jutted out to push aside the last tangle of branches.

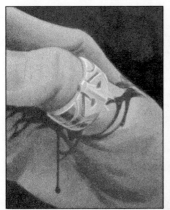

EIGHT

YOU . . .

YOU'RE HURT.

WILLOW, NO. LEAVE HIM... ALONE.

WHAT WAS HE DOING IN THERE?

DON'T EVEN THINK ABOUT IT, ASH. NOT HAPPENING.

I CAN FEEL IT. CALLING ME.

NINE

"ASH, WHAT JUST HAPPENED?" Willow asked.

Ash stared into the woods and tilted his head, as if trying to decipher a foreign language.

"Ash?" Willow said, louder this time. She gave him a backhanded tap on the shoulder. "Are you even listening?"

Ash shook his head, blinking away the cobwebs. "Yeah, what?"

Willow's eyes narrowed. "You okay?"

"Um . . ."

"Let's get out of here," Willow said. "Get back to the room."

"It's fine . . . I'm fine," Ash insisted.

"No, it's definitely *not* fine. Everything is weird and freaky and"—she pointed into the woods—"that place creeps me out like a bad middle school dance. The last thing I need is for *you* to start acting all strange with that glazed, zombified look in your eyes. Come on, Little Brother. We're leaving. Now."

Without a word of argument, Ash dutifully rose and followed his sister. He didn't even look back. Not once.

Ash knew he'd see it again.

Later in the room, Ash and Willow sat on the edges of their beds, facing each other. Ash took a long sip of ice water from a plastic cup. He held the empty cup in his hands, turning it slowly as they talked.

"You went in farther than I did," Willow said. "Did you see anything in the woods?"

Ash shrugged, shook his head. "It was dark and then I heard running, I guess. I wasn't sure what it was."

"Same," Willow said. "I thought it might have been a bear or a moose or—"

"A moose? Seriously?"

"Yeah," Willow said, smiling despite herself. "You don't want to get trampled by a moose, believe me. Those dudes are big."

"Oh, like you have experience?" Ash said.

"I watch a lot of YouTube. I know things."

"But it wasn't a moose. It was Kristoff," Ash said.

"And he was bleeding. And running. As if something had attacked him, and he was trying to get away," Willow said.

"Maybe. I don't know," Ash replied.

Willow watched as Ash kept twisting the cup in his fingers. There was something off about it, hypnotic. The cup revolving in his hands. He seemed different, changed in some way she couldn't quite identify. "Can you, like, stop with the cup. It's annoying." She snatched it from his hands and tossed it into the garbage can. Well, not exactly *into*. More like *reasonably close*. The cup bounced off the wall and rolled onto the carpet. It startled Daisy, who'd been lying on the floor, watching them, hoping for a walk.

Willow stood up. Daisy rose with her. "I'm going

to talk to Kristoff. Maybe he needs help. If you can, give Daisy a walk. Just don't go near those woods. And be careful of the main road. I've seen some big trucks hauling butt down there."

Ash looked up, smiled. *Hauling butt.* He liked that. Willow had a way with words. "What about Mom and Dad?"

Willow glanced at the door that connected their rooms. She pulled a hand across her lips. "Not a word. Okay?"

Ash yawned, suddenly sleepy. He wasn't used to being up at the crack of dawn. It all started with that screeching alarm. A slight headache formed behind his eyes. All things considered, he'd rather be sleeping.

When Willow reached the door, Ash heard himself say, "Careful, Will."

"Pish," Willow joked. "I mostly just want my money back from that vending machine. It's almost eight in the morning and I haven't had my breakfast Twizzlers yet."

The lobby was neat, everything in its place, but the overall vibe was one of neglect. Years of it. Slightly worn carpet, ugly colors on the walls and furnishings. Kristoff was seated behind the front desk, head down, reading. Willow didn't expect to see him back at work as if nothing had happened. Kristoff glanced up when Willow entered. His face was pale, his short hair stuck out in all directions, and he wore a large gauze bandage on his right cheek.

There were no other outward signs of injury.

"Hi," Willow said, suddenly tentative, unsure of herself. It was her first time alone with the boy.

He nodded, unsmiling.

An inner voice told her to be cautious. "So, um." Willow interlaced her fingers, palms out, stretching her arms. She came to the desk. Peered over. "What are you reading?"

Kristoff frowned and placed the paperback face-down on the desk. "Can I help you?"

"You don't have to get like that," Willow countered. "I only asked what you were reading. You know, it's a friendly sort of comment that normal people make to start conversations."

"Uh-huh," Kristoff said.

"Like, oh, for example . . . lovely weather we're

having . . . or how 'bout those Yankees . . . or, hmm, *what the heck happened to your face?*"

Kristoff reflexively touched the bandage. He gave no reply.

"So!" Willow said, her voice almost a shout. "How 'bout those Yankees?"

Kristoff shook his head. "I have a lot of work to do—"

"Yeah, reading a book," Willow said. "Some job you've got here. Anyway, for real, your dumb vending machine ate my money."

"Did you try to shake it?"

"Pushed it, rocked it, rolled it," Willow replied. "I would have turned it upside down and shook it, but I was in a hurry."

Kristoff opened a drawer and pulled out a zippered pouch. He counted out the change in quarters and dropped them into Willow's hand. "I'll speak with Mr. Do about the machine. He'll be in later today. Our apologies for the inconvenience."

"Am I supposed to know who that is?" Willow asked.

"Mr. Do is our employee. He's been with our

family for a long time. Mr. Do fixes things that are broken, keeps the grounds in order, paints rooms that need sprucing up."

Willow looked pointedly at the drab brown walls in the office. "From the looks of things, maybe you should call him 'Mr. Don't.' For starters, he could slop some paint around in here. You might try happy colors. Like turquoise or butterscotch or salmon."

"Salmon is a fish."

"It's a color, too." Willow paused. "Don't you look at clothing catalogs?"

Kristoff didn't answer. He leaned his chin in his left palm.

"Some air freshener would help, too," Willow suggested. "But don't use those little trees that hang in cars. Totally gross."

"Please write up your thoughts and leave them in the complaints box," Kristoff said.

Willow looked around. "I don't see one."

"Exactly."

Kristoff waited for Willow to leave.

Willow didn't move.

She noticed a plate of muffins. They looked

delicious. She wondered if they were for the guests. Probably, right? She felt a rumble in her belly. "How long did you say your family has owned this place?"

"I didn't say," Kristoff answered. He paused a beat. "It's been in our family for years. We've grown attached to the place."

Willow nodded. The thought made her sad. Maybe it was the way he said it. Like he was trapped or something. "Do you ever dream about moving away? You know, try the big city someday? Become a ski bum in the mountains? Buy a yurt and move to Mongolia?"

Kristoff's face changed for a moment. Something flashed in his eyes, but Willow couldn't read exactly what it meant. She had struck a nerve.

"Oh, we could never leave. Never, ever," Kristoff finally said a little mournfully. He folded his hands together. "The place has its charms. You'll see. We used to hire locals to clean the rooms, make the beds. Just part-time help. But we haven't been that busy the past few years. Town isn't what it used to be. Now I do most of it myself, in the summer, along with the help of Mr. Do."

"What about your mother?" Willow asked.

"You are full of questions," Kristoff said. He cleared his throat. "My mother's health . . . is not what it once was. She does the internet upkeep, the website. Billing, taxes, the business end of running a motel. I'm just the face at the front desk."

And a nice face it is, Willow thought. *Most definitely a very nice face.*

Willow shifted awkwardly on her feet. "So we saw you coming out of the woods."

"Yes, you did."

"There was blood on your hands. They were all scratched up."

Kristoff smiled. "You're exaggerating." He held up his hands. There was not a mark on them, not a single scratch or bruise.

"But—"

"What?"

"Your face," Willow said. "I saw it. Skin was hanging off. You'll need stitches."

Kristoff's fingertips went to the gauze covering. He picked at it with an index finger, lifted a flap, slowly peeled it off. There were three thin white lines, scarcely visible, ancient scars only a razor's edge in width.

"That's impossible." Willow stepped back. She ran her hands up from her forehead through her hair. "No one heals that fast. There were three gashes across your face just an hour ago."

TEN

"I THINK, PERHAPS, your mind has been playing tricks," Kristoff reasoned. "Yes, it's true, I acquired a few minor cuts. I used ointment, my mother's homemade solution. Nothing significant."

"It looked like something clawed at you—something wild."

Kristoff laughed. "Nothing that exciting, Willow. It's embarrassing, really. I enjoy running in the woods out back. They are known locally as the Whispering Pines. I carelessly slipped on a rock. That's it. No drama. No bear attacks. I slipped and fell."

"What were you doing out so early in the morning?"

"It's the best time of day, before my duties begin," Kristoff explained. "When the sun lifts over the horizon and the trees come alive with birdsong. Magical, don't you think?"

Kristoff's eyes slid over. Something attracted his attention outside the window. Willow saw that a red car had pulled up. The driver, a Black man, sat behind the wheel. A woman climbed out of the front passenger seat—she was attractive in a sheer blue top, with white shorts and dark, toned legs. A bright, multicolored headscarf completed the outfit. A back door opened and—*clank, clank*—a young girl stepped out. She, too, had her mother's features (the connection was obvious). Thick eyebrows, full lips, an alert, intelligent gaze. The slender girl walked using crutches with a cuff that wrapped loosely around her arms above the elbow. She must have been only eight or nine years old. She had an interesting way of getting around. She pushed the crutches in front of her, leaned forward, and used her hips, with a slight bend in the knees, to swing her legs through, both legs together in a single unit. She propelled herself forward with impressive skill and strength. Gathered herself again and again, moving forward like a talented gymnast on a pommel horse. Amazing, really, because it looked to Willow like neither of the girl's legs had much muscle. In fact, she noticed, there were rigid plastic braces keeping her ankles in place.

Willow stepped aside to watch them enter. She smiled at the girl, whose black hair was braided with colorful beads: orange, red, yellow, green, black, and brown. The girl beamed a smile right back, flashing two tidy rows of white teeth.

"Hello, hi, um—this is so awkward," the woman said, using her hands expressively. She had elegant long, thin fingers. A dozen bracelets jangled off her wrists. "I realize it's early and you probably don't even have rooms ready at this hour. But we've been driving all night and"—she paused, catching her breath—"I'm sorry, it's been a hard trip. Our nerves are a bit frayed."

Kristoff stood and smiled warmly. "There's nothing to apologize for, I assure you. Can I get you something? A cup of coffee? Tea? A muffin, perhaps?"

The woman turned to her daughter. "Juss, would you like a muffin? You said you were hungry."

"With chocolate chips," Kristoff offered.

"Yes, yum, thank you," Juss said, deftly moving to the counter.

Kristoff turned to the woman. "As a matter of fact, we do have rooms clean and immediately available. We can get you settled right away."

"Oh, that's wonderful. We're just exhausted. We were driving and driving all night—there was thick fog—and we saw your sign."

Willow's ears perked up.

Kristoff lifted his chin, indicating the car idling outside. "No pets, I see?"

The woman shook her head. She looked at her daughter, Justice (Juss for short), with kindness in her eyes. "No, no pets, I'm afraid. We recently lost our beautiful cat, Mission."

"Just last week," Justice said. "He slept on my pillow every night."

Kristoff clucked sympathetically. "Mission, that's an

interesting name." He swiveled to the computer and his fingers began racing across the keyboard. "Excuse me one moment," Kristoff said to the woman. He spoke in a different tone to Willow. "Was there anything else, er, miss?"

Willow took the hint. "No, no, I'm all good. I was just heading out." Willow pointed both thumbs at the door. With a quick move, she twirled and reached for the plate of muffins to snatch one up. Willow winked at the girl. "I like 'em with choco-late chips, too!"

As Willow reached the door, Kristoff called out, "Stephen King."

Willow turned, confused.

"The book. It's by Stephen King," he explained.

"Oh," Willow replied. "Sounds like fun. Horror, right?"

"My favorite genre," Kristoff said with a smile. "And remember, the Whispering Pines are not for you, Willow. It's infested with ticks. You don't want to get Lyme disease. Best to stay away."

"No worries," Willow replied. "We're leaving today, anyway."

Kristoff half smiled, as if he'd be happy to see them go.

Willow stepped outside. The sky was periwinkle blue. One dainty cloud drifted past. It was going to be a beautiful day. When Willow glanced back toward the office, Justice grinned and, eyes wide, gleefully shoved the entire muffin into her mouth. *Chomp!*

ELEVEN

ASH WAS ZONKED OUT, lying diagonally on top of his bed, blankets tossed to the side. Daisy, however, was wide awake. Tail thumping, eagerly nosing Willow the moment she opened the door. The dog whined softly.

"Okay, shhh-shhh, let's go for a walk," she told the long-legged goldendoodle. Willow clipped the leash on Daisy's collar and stepped back outside.

The motel was situated on a small hill tucked away from the main road. A long entranceway led to the parking lot and main building. There was plenty of open space for grass and a surprisingly pretty rock garden to explore. To the right, surrounded by a wrought-iron fence, was the pool with a good-size shed filled with, Willow guessed, your typical pool stuff. Behind that there was a small pavilion with scattered chairs and a couple of picnic tables.

From outside the fence, Willow snapped a few artistic photos of the annoyingly empty cement pool.

It was already shaping up to be a hot day, and that useless pool only served to irritate Willow. The gate swung open in the breeze—unlocked, or more likely broken. A job for Mr. Do. A funny name for a motel handyman. She got a kick out of that name. Maybe she should lay out, anyway, work on the tan. She had a cute new bathing suit she hadn't even worn yet.

Oh yeah. They were leaving today.

Willow thought about Kristoff's vanishing scar. Was he right? Had she been exaggerating his injuries? No, Ash saw it, too. How could Kristoff's cuts have healed so quickly? A mystery. It gnawed at her. Willow didn't like loose ends. She wanted all the facts to line up in a neat row. Did she believe his story about slipping on a rock? It seemed reasonable.

People run and slip all the time. It's perfectly normal. But clearly, the answer was no. Kristoff was lying.

Willow didn't completely trust Daisy off leash, particularly not in a new place—and not with the traffic zipping past on the road below. She watched a big truck rumble past, and it gave her a shiver. Just the thought of it, her sweet dog hit by a vehicle. How awful. Daisy tugged in the other direction, toward the back of the building, but no way was Willow going toward the woods. Bad vibes over there.

After Daisy did her business, Willow softly knocked on her parents' door. Mrs. McGinn smiled warmly, kneeled down to let Daisy lick her face, and murmured sweet nothings. Willow could see her father sitting in a chair, head cocked oddly to the side. He wasn't smiling, didn't greet her. Something was wrong.

Willow gestured with a chin lift. "What's up with Dad?"

Mrs. McGinn glanced back, stepped forward, and closed the door behind her. "There's been a change of plans," she explained. "We need to stay a little longer."

"Stay? Here?"

"Your father seems to have hurt his neck during last night's fire drill fiasco. This morning, it's gotten worse," Willow's mother said. "I'm going to run into town and get ice packs and Tylenol. Maybe a heating pad? I'll try to make an appointment with a doctor. Or maybe just a good physical therapist? I don't really know what's available around here."

"You think he's, like . . . hurt bad?" Willow was worried, and it came through in her voice.

"No, no, nothing like that," Mrs. McGinn said. "He just needs rest, maybe some muscle relaxers if I can find a doctor to write a prescription. He's not up for a long car ride. I hope you and Ash are not too disappointed?" She looked around the dreary Exit 13 Motel, the underwhelming (and nearly empty) parking lot. "I know this isn't the trip we'd hoped for—"

"We're fine, Mom, really, don't worry about us. I mean, another day of deathless boredom isn't going to bother us," Willow said. "I've already experienced a full year of middle school, so I've had plenty of practice."

Mrs. McGinn smiled, waggled the key fob, and

said, "Well, I'm going into town. I won't be too long—and I'll try to come back with some breakfast and cold cuts for lunch, maybe something fun for dinner. There's a mini fridge in our room to keep things fresh."

"And a big box of Dots," Willow suggested.

"We'll see about the Dots," Mrs. McGinn replied. "Want to come?"

"Um, I'm good." Willow suppressed a yawn. "I'm going to stick around here—I don't know—torture Ash or something."

"That sounds constructive," Mrs. McGinn said with a laugh. She enjoyed her daughter's dark humor.

Willow waved as the car pulled away. Daisy whined.

Another day in Nowhereland.

Five miles south of Dullsville.

That is, it was dull for Willow—until the bizarre, smelly rabbits showed up. At least, according to Ash.

That's what he said.

He told her they only come out at night.

TWELVE

IT WASN'T THAT Ash didn't like people. People were *fine,* mostly. Ash had always gotten along with his class- mates and was invited to all the right birthday parties. But Ash never once had a best friend. In fact, if he were asked to name his closest friend on the planet, his mind would go blank. There would be no answer. There was no special friend.

Ash shrugged it away. A close friend wasn't some- thing he needed or desired. In truth, Ash held a private reserve that separated him from others. Maybe his classmates sensed it, a protective bubble through which there was no entry.

Ash never felt lonely, just alone.

Alone in the world.

Except for Willow and Daisy and his parents. Ash wasn't sure if family counted. He loved them, of course. But there was always a distance that was hard to explain—a separateness, *an otherness*, as if he were a creature from another dimension. An outsider even within his own family. Ash operated in his own self-contained universe. And if it ever bothered him, if Ash ever felt a pang of solitude, *of sadness*, the feeling soon drifted away like wind-blown fog.

Ash was happiest, he told himself, when he was alone.

Like now.

He walked across the parking lot. Ash scrambled to the top of a low rock wall that separated the black-top from the lawn beyond. Ash stood with his back to the motel. He slowed his breathing, calmly filled his lungs, and exhaled. He closed his eyes. Ash soon sensed a familiar tingling in his fingertips, spreading into his hands, then up into his arms, until his entire body vibrated like the wings of a hummingbird. He then sensed a weight pressing down upon his right shoulder, like the firm hand of a stranger. But it wasn't a hand—not a hand at all. A presence, then. A connection.

Something there.

Ash turned and found that he was alone.

Always alone.

He stared across at the Exit 13 Motel, and the building seemed to stare back at him. Ash felt a strange sensation. Like he was on the edge of an awareness that he couldn't put into words. He asked aloud of the old motel, "Tell me. What are you? Why do you make me feel like I'm vibrating?"

A car arrived to break the spell. Ash blinked and squinted in the bright and hazy sunlight.

He decided to make a slow inspection of the building. He began by circling it, noting every door and window. A laundry room filled with two industrial washing machines and dryers. A supply closet. The ice and vending machines. The office with its floor-to-ceiling windows, and sixteen guest rooms numbered 1 to 16. And there between rooms 7 and 8, an unnumbered door. Ash paused by a window with drawn, thick curtains. He listened. The whirring of an air conditioner. A clink of ice in a glass. Some instinct caused Ash to check the knob. It was locked.

Did the curtain flutter?

Was someone inside?

Ash hurried away.

A rhyme came into his mind:

> *"Ring-a-round the rosie,*
> *a pocketful of posies,*
> *Ashes! Ashes!*
> *We all fall down."*

It was an old folk song that Ash had heard his entire life. That's what happens when your parents name you after a tree: People sing that song to you. Ash actually liked his name. It was different but not *too different*. It was better than being named, oh, Dogwood or Beech. Come to think of it, Beech might have been a cool name. Especially if you were a surfer (Ash wasn't; he had a thing about sharks and not wanting to be eaten by them).

Anyway, that song had earwormed into his skull at an early age, and it popped up, willy-nilly, at random times. It was nearing twilight. His mother had discovered a rusted-out grill and the splintery picnic tables on the far side of the pool. So she fired up some briquettes and would soon be grilling burgers and "making things nice" for everyone. Ash's dad rested inside room 16, groggy from muscle relaxers. Ash easily drifted away unnoticed, like a leaf blown by the breeze.

He didn't plan on going into the woods. But something drew him close, faint murmurings and whispers, so he came to a little cove of dry yellow grass three-quarters surrounded by a dense thicket of shrubs. He sat cross-legged, leaning back on his hands, and waited for dusk to fall across his shoulders. The blanket of night dropping down. His favorite time, when light gave way to darkness. The gloaming hour.

In that stillness, the voices reached his ears. Ash listened as they whispered their dark secrets. A dusky gray rabbit poked out of the woods, nibbling at the grass. Then another, and another. The largest rabbit— the first one—was unusually large. It stared directly at Ash. Its eyes were bloodred, like no rabbit the boy

Was this what the forest meant for him to see?

A wind blew, stirring the tall pines. They bent and swooned. A black crow cried, lifted off. And more, five, eight, a dozen crows swooped and circled. Suddenly, one flew down, talons outstretched, and hit Ash in the scalp. Shocked, he staggered back to regain his balance. More crows dove and swooped. Ash's scalp stung. He touched it. There was blood on his hands. More screaming crows came in for the attack.

THIRTEEN

A MEMORY FLOODED BACK. The first time the terror gripped him, when Ash was just a small boy. Maybe three or four years old. He was in bed at night in his own room. It was a thrilling time. At first, he had shared a bedroom with Willow. Then his family moved to a larger apartment so that both children could have rooms of their own.

Ash lay on his back, a little boy in a big-boy bed swimming in the murky darkness. The door was ajar, the way he insisted; a light from the hallway leaked into the room. The bedroom window was half open, and with a gust, the sheer white curtains billowed. The door banged shut.

All the light died with it.

Young Ash lay trembling, two small hands gripping the blanket, eyes watchful. That's when the noises started. Clawing, scraping, murmuring. Ash listened, muscles rigid, almost unable to breathe. He wanted to cry out, "Mom! Dad! Willow!" But his throat felt constricted, tight as a fist. No sound left his lips. Like he'd swallowed sand.

The room grew cold.

So very cold.

That's when an old voice, scratchy and parched, began to softly sing: "*Ashes, ashes, we all fall down.*"

The voice was under his bed.

Go away, Ash thought. *I don't want you here.*

People talk about chests pounding with fear. The *thump-thump-thump* of terror. But it was not like that for Ash. He felt hollowed out, empty, a husk. Perfectly still. If his heart beat, it was as silent as a grave.

"Ashhhhh," the voice hissed. "Come into the dark. There's work to be done. Hurry now, little one."

Bump. His mattress rose and fell.

Still Ash could not cry out.

The curtain billowed as if something invisible—something dark and terrible—had crawled into the room.

I won't, Ash thought.

"You will," the voice answered, crackling like dry leaves.

Ash felt but did not see—for his eyes were now closed tight—a hand, a claw, a bony thing reach up the side of his bed. The covers shifted; they were being pulled to the floor.

Ash held on tight.

I won't let go, I won't, he struggled.

"One day," the voice said, "you will help make things right."

"No," Ash said, his voice a muted whisper.

Scratch, scratch. The sound of claws on wooden floors. "We will watch you in the dark and wait for you, always, Ashhhhh," the sibilant voice slurred. "Ashes to ashes, dust to dust—until we all are returned to our rightful places."

That's when Ash found his voice again.

And he used it . . . to SCREAM.

A high howl of horror.

His parents came running.

They held him and gave him water and patted his back and said, "There, there," and "There, there."

And they told Ash that he was only imagining things.

It was all nothing, nothing at all.

Ash learned his lesson that night.

After that, he stopped telling his parents about the monster under the bed, the scary creatures in the woods, and the ancient trees that talked and somehow knew his name.

Ash never once thought of it as special.

Or a gift.

FOURTEEN

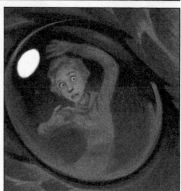

Asssssshhhhh.

Dazed, Ash began to sit up. He leaned on one hand, looking at the old, thin Asian man.

"Who—"

"What did you do? What did you see?" the man asked.

Ash tilted his head. The man looked away, his eyes scanning the area. There was intelligence in his gaze—an alertness—but also anxiety, fear. He wore khaki trousers, a light blue work shirt buttoned to the collar, and a green John Deere baseball cap. A whisk broom, his weapon, lay on the grass. A ring of keys looped to his belt. And a knife in its sheath.

"You rest," the man said. He gently but firmly eased Ash back to the ground. "Better to lie down. Rest a few minutes."

Ash complied. He became aware of a throbbing ache, like a bass drum pounding out a harsh rhythm. He reached for the tender spot at the top of his head. It felt raw, squishy, wet.

"Let me see," the man said.

"Who—" Ash repeated.

"Mr. Do," the man said. "Maintenance man. I

work here. Heard the crows. They protect their nests."

He probed Ash's wound, pressing lightly with his fingers. "You'll be all right. Clean it out, soap and water. Use antiseptic." And again he asked, "What else did you see?"

Ash lay on the grass while the stranger, Mr. Do, examined his scalp. A bizarre scene, but he felt safe, protected. "Rabbits," Ash said. "Really weird, freaky rabbits."

Mr. Do made no response. If he thought that was strange, he didn't say so.

"The crows, all above me, black wings, diving—"

"Crows are territorial," the old man explained. "Very protective. Very common this time of year, very good parents, nothing to think about."

Then Ash remembered. "And a wolf! Yeah, a big wolf—the same one I saw before. It was huge, and it watched me from the trees. It held a kitten in its mouth. It said my name—"

At the mention of the wolf, Mr. Do closed his eyes. He tilted his head to the sky. He took a long, slow, deep breath. A sort of sigh. He shook his hands in a sort of momentary spasm. Rubbed them on the grass.

Then he placed his left hand on Ash's shoulder and collarbone. He squeezed, his strong fingertips digging in. "Sleep now, forget," he said.

Mr. Do pressed his right thumb against the base of Ash's skull where it met the top of his neck. The old man counted, three, two, one.

The boy drifted off into unconsciousness.

FIFTEEN

"ASH, WAKE UP."

Willow gently shook Ash's shoulder.

She shook him again, this time not half as gently.

"I was looking all over for you. It's almost time to eat."

Ash sat up groggily. A few blades of grass were stuck to his chin. He wiped drool from his mouth.

"Jesus, Ash, you were out like a light," Willow said. "What were you thinking? Sleeping out here?"

"I—I don't know . . ." he said. His brain was fuzzy.

"You're lucky I found you," Willow said.

Ash yawned. He glanced to the sky. Stars had begun to appear, tiny pinpricks of light. A sickle moon climbed over Willow's right shoulder. He rubbed his eyes, ran his hands through his tousled blond hair, and felt the wound on his head. "Ouch," he said.

Willow leaned in for a look-see. "Whoa."

"How bad?"

Will snapped a photo and showed it to him. Asked, "Did you fall?"

"I don't remember," he confessed.

His thoughts were shapeless, formless. A knot of loose strings impossible to unravel. Before handing the phone back to Willow, he instinctively took a photo of the woods in front of them.

A cold, damp feeling suddenly came over him—like passing through a cool spot in a swimming pool. He shivered. At that instant, the cold spot *seemed to pass through him.*

As if . . . as if a ghost walked through.

Goose bumps appeared on his skin.

"You're cold?" Willow asked.

He nodded. "Aren't you?"

"Uh, yeah, not at all. It's warm out, LB. Let me see your eyes. Look at me," Willow ordered. She peered into his eyes. They didn't seem cloudy or unfocused or unusual in any way. "Looks okay to me. Probably nothing."

Probably nothing, nothing at all.

Ash had heard those words before.

Willow took a few more photos of Ash. No reason, really. Just to document the moment. She was into that lately. This happened. Then this happened. Then this other thing happened. Photo, photo, photo. Maybe make a scrapbook someday. Title it *Pictures from My Boring Trip to Exit 13 Motel.*

Ash rubbed the back of his neck, the spot where his spine met the skull. It gave him a numb, tingling sensation, like when a foot falls asleep. His belly rumbled, a sudden sharp tug of hunger. He reached out a hand. "Here, help me up."

They clasped each other at the forearm, and Willow pulled. "Come on. Mom's called a family meeting. But first, go wash up. Fix your hair. And change your shirt. You look like roadkill."

"Real nice," Ash replied.

"Roasted," Willow said, grinning.

Mrs. McGinn stood by the picnic table, spatula in hand, watching for their arrival. Ash could almost hear the fat from the burgers sizzling on the grill. Daisy, attached to a long leash, sat up expectantly. She let out the softest whine, longing to be touched, hugged, loved. There were a few floodlights in the pool and picnic areas. Their mother had found a red-and-white-checkered tablecloth in town and laid out an assortment of paper plates and plastic cups. Potato salad, watermelon, chips, lemonade, a citronella candle to keep away the mosquitoes.

"Glad you could make it," she said to Ash.

"I found him crashed out on the grass," Willow told her mother. "Fast asleep!"

Mrs. McGinn looked at her son. "Are you feeling all right?"

"Oh yeah," Ash said with a shrug. "I was relaxing and, I don't know, just drifted off." He bent down to pet Daisy, rubbing her neck and shoulders. She especially liked a scratch right behind the ears. Ash paused, looking around. "Where's Dad?"

"Inside resting, watching old *Twilight Zone* episodes

on TV. He found an oldies station. I'll check on him in a minute. The painkillers—the medication—help relax the muscles in his neck. But they also make him veeeerrrrryyyy sleeeeepy," their mother explained, imitating an old-time hypnotist.

She set out a plate of cheeseburgers—the McGinns were enthusiastically a cheeseburger family—only maniacs wouldn't want cheese on their burgers—and Willow said, "I like eating late like this. In the dark. Summer is fun like that. It's like, I don't know, time changes. It gets stretched out like Silly Putty. Not like winter, when everything's all squished together and it gets late so early."

Ash liked that about his sister. Willow came out with the weirdest, most unexpected observations. She had an interesting mind. *It gets late early.* And she was right. The lazy days of summer really did last longer. Time here at Exit 13 Motel felt different. The rush and push of everyday life had slipped away. And here they were, eating dinner at nine at night.

"Lo and behold, here comes your father now," Mrs. McGinn said. She watched her husband closely, a measure of concern on her face.

Mr. McGinn walked gingerly out to the picnic area. He gave a quick, automatic wave. He held his body stiffly, as if he were made of glass. He wore a beige neck brace that Mrs. McGinn had picked up at the local convenience store. The children watched as their father cautiously lowered himself with a grimace into a metal chair beside the picnic table. Mrs. McGinn fussed over him, placing a rolled-up towel behind his head. "Is that okay? Is this better? Would you rather be back inside? Can I do anything for you, honey?"

He looked up at her by shifting his eyes without moving his head. Unable to nod, not eager even to talk, he raised a thumb. All good.

Willow and Ash exchanged glances.

He didn't seem like his usual chipper self.

They began to eat in silence.

"So what did you want to tell us?" Ash asked.

"I'm going to the hospital tomorrow," Mr. McGinn piped up. All eyes turned to him. "A minor procedure. They are removing my head and replacing it with a coconut."

"A coconut? That might be useful if we get thirsty,"

Willow joked. "Crack it open and glug, glug, glug."

Ash looked at her and frowned.

"What?" she said. "We can't joke?"

Mrs. McGinn placed her two hands on the table. "We couldn't get your father in for an MRI today. There was a problem with the machine. Supposedly it will be fixed first thing in the morning. And, truthfully, I don't want to put your father through a long, uncomfortable drive until we know the severity of his injury."

"Sweetie pie, pumpkin, I'll be fine," Mr. McGinn meekly protested. "I can rest in the car and—"

"Spinal injuries are nothing to fool with. So we'll stay here for another day or two," Mrs. McGinn announced, cutting off her husband's protests. "It's decided." She looked from Willow to Ash. "I'm sorry. *We're* sorry. Your father feels terrible. This is not the road trip we'd hoped to give you kids. Any questions?"

"So, like, we're stuck here," Willow said. "Exit 13 Motel. My friends will be so jealous."

"Hush, Will," Ash said. "Dad's hurt. Don't be selfish."

Willow began to say something in protest—caught a look from her mother—and decided against it. They were stuck here. At least the TV had 477 channels.

She'd counted.

SIXTEEN

THE AIR CONDITIONER rattled and hummed but never quite got the room cool. Just noisier. Ash and Willow lay faceup on their beds, using only thin sheets for cover. Daisy rested on a blanket on the floor between them. The lights were out.

Willow thumbed through her phone, looking at old photos, playing with the edit features. "You awake?"

Ash groaned a yes.

"The cutest girl came to the motel today while I was talking to Kristoff," Willow said. "She had these bright, colorful beads in her hair. Her smile was amazing. Dimples. So sweet."

"How old is she?"

Willow laughed at an old photo, a friend's face covered in vanilla ice cream. "Can't say," she answered distractedly. "Eight, nine? There was something going on with her legs. But you should have seen her with those crutches. She could get around, no problem. I liked her right away. She reminded me of an Olympic gymnast the way she handled them. It was pretty awesome overall."

Willow continued, "I wonder what's up with her? If I see her tomorrow, I'll have to ask."

"Do you think you should?" Ash asked. "Maybe it's better not to talk about it."

Willow pondered that. "No," she decided. "I think it's better to talk about things. Be open and honest. What am I going to do? Pretend she's not standing there on crutches? Act like everything's perfectly normal and we can go ride bicycles together?"

"Maybe she doesn't want to feel different?" Ash reasoned. He honestly didn't know the right answer. Sometimes it was hard to know.

"The same thing happened to her family that

happened to us. They got lost driving around, saw the sign, and ended up here," Willow said.

"*Hmm*," Ash said.

"Hey!" Willow said excitedly. "I never told you about my meeting with Kristoff!"

"Oh right," Ash said. "What did you call him? Your vampire sweetie? I can't believe that slipped my mind. It's like my brain's been glitching all day."

"First of all, it's vampire *hottie*. Secondly, he was almost completely healed. Hardly any cuts at all."

"His face looked pretty torn up when he came out of the woods," Ash said. "Maybe he covered them up?"

"I guess," Willow conceded, suddenly doubting herself. "He could have worn concealer or . . . um . . . gross . . . I think Daisy just farted."

Ash sniffed. "It smells like something died in here. Are you sure it wasn't you?"

"No way!" Willow said. "I only fart rainbows and daffodils and cupcakes with sprinkles."

Ash rolled his eyes. *Where does she come up with this stuff?* "Tell me more about Kristoff. What did he say?"

"Not a lot," Willow said. "But there was one

thing—I keep playing it over in my head—it just struck me as weird. He said, 'The Whispering Pines are not for you, Willow.'"

"What's the weird part?"

"It was the way he said it. He was in the woods, right? He said he liked to run on the trails, that he slipped and fell. Okay, sure, whatever. But he said it was full of ticks. If that was true, what was he doing in there?"

Ash pictured Kristoff as he left the woods. He wore long pants and boots. Good tick protection, but a lousy outfit for running. *The Whispering Pines are not for you, Willow.* Ash heard that line differently. He silently asked himself, *Who, then, are they for?*

Ash wondered, not for the first time, if the woods were meant for him. Not for Willow—but for Ash. He couldn't imagine a reason why that might be true. And yet . . . it felt true in his bones.

Ash offered up a lame observation: "Kristoff's an unusual guy."

"I'll say!" Willow agreed. "So mysterious. I mean, did you check out that thumb ring? How many guys wear thumb rings with a wolf carved into it?"

Something stirred in Ash's brain. A memory breaking loose, like a portion of an ice glacier calving into the sea. The wolf with a white kitten in its mouth.

"I remember now. I saw the wolf again. It's a dire wolf."

Willow rose up on an elbow. "You did? When?"

"Right before you found me. There were rabbits, too. But something was wrong with them. A bad smell. They seemed—and I know you'll think this is crazy—dangerous."

"Crazy? Oh, no, not me," Willow countered. "Killer rabbits. That's totally normal."

Ash shot her a look.

"I'm sorry, LB," Willow apologized. "But it's pretty far-fetched. And I didn't see a wolf."

"You don't believe anything I say. You never have," Ash fumed.

Willow took a slow, deep breath. She wanted to choose her words carefully. "We've been through this before, Ash. You know how it is. You've always had an—"

"Active imagination," he said, completing her sentence. "I'm so tired of hearing that."

"It's true, though, isn't it?" shot back Willow. "Monsters in the attic. Angry gnomes running around."

"Ha! Angry gnomes?! I never saw an angry gnome in my life!"

"Right, I forgot. All the gnomes you know are happy-happy," Willow teased.

They lay in the dark, the rattle of the air-conditioning the only sound. Daisy gave a low, soft ruff and twitched her paws, running in her sleep. It was better than farting.

"What's a dire wolf, anyway?" Willow asked.

"I don't know. It's just . . . what it . . . told me."

"You talked to it?"

"No, I can't—it's hard to explain," Ash replied. "I know how this sounds to you, Will. But I receive her messages."

"Her thoughts? She's a girl?"

"Yes, I think so."

"And you are like a satellite dish," Willow said, "receiving signals?"

"I guess," Ash said.

"Well? What did your make-believe wolf want?"

"Don't be like that," Ash pleaded.

Ash wanted to say more, but for some reason, he held his tongue. *The wolf wanted me to take the white cat.* Yeah, explaining that to Willow would be too weird.

Willow heard the hurt in his voice. Maybe she made fun of his imaginary creatures too often. He was such an easy target, though! But still, she didn't want to hurt his feelings. She made a silent vow to be gentler with him, more understanding—even if he was sometimes just a lovable whackjob.

Drip, drip, drip, leaked the faucet. A new annoyance. Willow kept scrolling through the photos. Playing with the filters, brightening, trying different tints, recropping, editing. Almost to the end of the library. She had caught up to today. Some flowers. Shuffleboard with her mom. Action shots of her dad propped up with pillows in bed. Ash asleep in the grass. The bump on his—

She stopped, looked closer, enlarged the photo with a flick of her fingers. It was the photo Ash had taken of the woods. She added a filter, another. Tweaked the contrast, vibrancy, shadows, and sharpness. Reduced the noise.

Willow sat up, stunned, almost unable to catch her breath.

"Oh my god. Ash! I'm so sorry. I'm so, so sorry."

"What?"

"I didn't believe you."

"What?" he repeated.

"I think I found your wolf."

She sat beside her brother. "Look," she explained, fingers moving expertly.

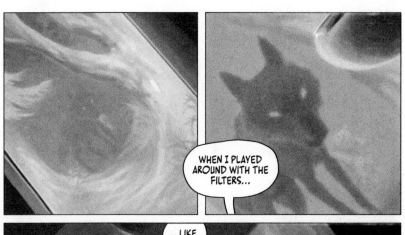

WHEN I PLAYED AROUND WITH THE FILTERS...

...LIKE THIS.

THERE'S MY WOLF. STARING RIGHT AT ME.

YOU WEREN'T IMAGINING THINGS AFTER ALL.

SEVENTEEN

WHILE THE CHILDREN SLEPT and the faucet dripped, Daisy remained ill at ease. The dog rose, stirred, pawed at the blanket, circled, plopped down again. Sighed the way only a dog can sigh. With its whole entire being.

Unable to rest.

She was upset by the scratching in the walls.

The strong smells therein.

Creatures clawing, scratching, scraping, gnawing to get inside.

The growling and yowling and howling in the near woods.

The low voices in the trees.

Daisy stood and patrolled the baseboards, sniffed the walls, inhaled all the scents and nocturnal activities. Imagined what was haunting the grounds outside, growling in time to the night's mystic music.

Something dark and ominous out there. Creatures big and small. Alive and undead. Daisy knew it and was afraid.

If she had the words, Daisy would say: *The sharp-toothed wolf prowls the grounds.*

Daisy had seen enough of Exit 13 Motel.

It was time to go . . .

First chance she got . . .

Home.

EIGHTEEN

THE WOLF CAME again that night. Ash awoke to its claws clicking on the cement pathway outside. So he rose and slipped out into the night. Shutting the door behind him, he glimpsed Willow asleep in bed. Mouth open, one arm dangling down. Daisy lifted her head, watched with alarm as the boy left the room.

No wind stirred. To his left, he saw the high-shouldered wolf saunter past the rooms toward the office at the far end of the building. Its bushy, black-tipped tail hung straight down. The wolf paused and looked back over its shoulder at Ash through almond-shaped eyes as if to ask: *Are you coming?* Ash waited, dazed and entranced, his hand still on the doorknob. A hundred thousand pinpricks of light crowded the night sky. Finally the creature turned . . . and walked *through* the closed door . . . right through it! . . . and was gone.

Ash walked past the row of rooms until he came to the unnumbered door. It was impossible but, also, true. Ash saw what he saw. He felt the knob. This time, it was left unlocked. He cautiously pushed the door open. He stood motionless, waiting for his eyes to adjust to the dark. Entering the room, he made certain the heavy curtains were closed. He went to the standing lamp in the corner and, pulling on a cord, risked the light.

The bulb gave off a warm glow.

Ash instantly saw that the room was empty. If he had been correct—if the wolf had truly entered *through* the door—somehow it was here no longer. Still, he smelled it—the musky, foresty odor of a wild animal. The room was unlike the other guest rooms. At least, the ones he'd seen—rooms 15 and 16. Ash assumed they were all alike. This room had no bed, for starters. In the corner to his right, there was a large stuffed chair beside a free-standing reading lamp. The lamp was old-fashioned, with a metal pole. The shade was made of stained glass. There was a small table with an empty water glass and book. Bookshelves stood along the back wall from floor to ceiling.

The only other piece of furniture was a large wooden wardrobe. Ash opened it. The closet contained empty shelves, along with a bar for hanging clothes. Oddly, there was a ceramic bowl on the floor, filled with water. Ash shut the doors. He stepped back to examine it. The piece did not make sense; it was an odd, boxy object to cram into a small room. Ash noticed small clumps of dirt on the carpet, clearly made by footprints. Human footprints. He moved deeper into the room, opened a door, and found the bathroom. It smelled of ammonia and was sparkling clean. So that was it. A library—*no, a reading room*—and a clunky wooden wardrobe that took up far too much space. Ash's attention returned to the bookshelf. Along the left panel, the image of a leaping wolf had been carved into the wood. The wolf was jumping over water, which was depicted by curving lines. Above it, a constellation of stars and planets.

He picked up the book under the reading lamp. It was large and heavy. The cover showed only bold capital letters stacked oddly:

THE BOO
KOFLIM
INA
LSPAC
ES

There was no author's name.

A code? Ash wondered. *Words squished together? The spaces in wrong places?*

He puzzled it over in his mind. *The book of . . . ? Limi? Limin?*

In a . . . spaces?

Liminal spaces?

◊◊◊

Ash had no idea what that word *liminal* even meant. Was it a real word? He'd have to look it up later. He flipped through the pages, noting chapters that read:

"Passageways and Thresholds," "Transitions," "Visitors from Beyond," "Susurrations and Whispers," and "Unanticipated Dangers."

A scrap of paper fell out of the book and onto the floor. Ash bent to pick it up. Someone had hastily scribbled in ancient cursive, THE KEY: WHAT SENSES DO WE LACK??!!

Ash set the book back down. He returned to the carving of the wolf. It felt significant somehow. Meaningful. He ran his fingers over it, touching the wolf's snout, sharp upturned ears, long limbs, powerful paws—when, *click*, the wardrobe door opened behind him.

Ash froze in fear. He stared at the door, half expecting someone to step through it. Nothing stirred. Finally Ash pulled the door all the way open. The closet was transformed. No shelves, no rod, no water bowl. It had all vanished. But on the floor, there was a thick metal ring. A nylon cord was attached to it, knotted at the end. A secret hatch built into the floor!

Footsteps sounded from outside, heavy boots on cement.

Ash scanned the room, heart hammering. *Where to hide?*

At that instant, perhaps in response to Ash's question, the book's pages began to flutter. But there was no wind in the room, no ceiling fan, no breeze. Still the pages fluttered and flicked and finally flew open to a new spread. Ash stepped to the book, craning his neck to read. There was so little time. The footsteps drew closer. The chapter read, "The Art of Camouflage."

The footsteps stopped. A key entered a lock.

Ash closed his eyes, tilted his head up, and felt his tongue roll back into his throat.

His heart slowed.

He breathed through the pores of his skin.

It felt as if he were reptilian, a desert creature disappearing into itself.

The door opened.

Kristoff stood at the entranceway. His eyes searched the empty room. A finger went to his tooth. "Mother?" he whispered. "Mother? Are you in here? Answer me, please."

He frowned at the freestanding lamp. Kristoff

strode to it and abruptly turned off the light with a sharp tug on the pull string. The room plunged into full dark. Kristoff sighed with weariness. Ash could hear the tiniest sound, and he felt the ripples of air swirl around him. Kristoff hissed, stepped back outside, and yanked the door shut.

Ash was alone again.

And somehow, amazingly, he was also invisible.

Camouflaged like a chameleon.

Once again he smelled it. The near, musky odor of wolf.

Minutes later, after he returned to his normal self, Ash fled the room. He felt frightened and disoriented. *What had happened to him? What was this place?* In his haste, Ash left the book behind. *I won't tell Willow,* he told himself. *Not yet. No, I won't tell anyone . . . for now.*

NINETEEN

IN THE MORNING, Ash lingered in bed, thinking about the night's events. The room, the book, Kristoff, and the wolf. *Had he truly turned himself invisible?*

Willow sang in the shower, loudly and badly. She came out, drying her hair with a towel. "You all good, LB?" she asked cheerily.

"What? Oh sure, peachy," Ash answered.

Willow said it was time to take Daisy out to do her business. It was part of the family arrangement. Let the parents sleep. There was a strip of grass, just downslope, that had become her spot. They stood around, dawdling, waiting for Daisy, who seemed intent on sniffing every rock, plant, and blade of grass.

From the far end of the building, an older Korean man dressed in jeans and a sturdy blue button-down shirt, sleeves folded up to the forearms, pushed a cart with one hand. He lugged a wooden ladder under his other arm. The man moved slowly but gracefully, walking lightly on the balls of his feet.

He wore headphones and might have been bouncing along to a hip-hop tune. "That must be the famous Mr. Do," Willow murmured.

Ash followed his sister's gaze. The man was thin and not tall, with a lean jaw and short gray-black hair. The cart contained a large garbage can and other items—a vacuum, a whisk broom, towels, sheets, and cleaning supplies. "You've met him before?" Ash asked.

"No, um," Willow said absently, "Kristoff mentioned him. Some kind of handyman who helps out around the place."

"Seems so."

"I like his name: *Mr. Do*."

Seemingly unaware of being observed, the

maintenance man knocked on the door of room 15. Receiving no answer—the room was empty after all—he took out a set of keys, knocked again, this time pulled off his headphones, called out something they couldn't make out, and opened the door.

It felt odd to see a stranger enter their room. But moments later, he exited with a small garbage pail. Mr. Do dumped it into the large gray bin and returned the empty pail with a new plastic lining to the room. He moved on for another few steps, then stopped in his tracks. He stared down at the ground. Looked left, looked right, as if to make sure no one was watching. He bent down and picked up a piece of hose or rubber or—

Mr. Do tossed it into the bin.

Before Ash could form the question, Willow asked out loud, "Was that a snake? Did Mr. Do just pick up a pretty massive snake and throw it in the garbage? Let's check it out."

She tugged the leash and Ash followed.

Mr. Do saw the children coming, half dragging a reluctant dog. He again set down the ladder. "You must be room fifteen?"

"That's right," Willow said, smiling. "Our parents are in room sixteen, next door. My name is Willow, and this is my brother, Ash."

Mr. Do nodded politely. "And your dog's name?"

"Daisy," Willow answered. "I know, it's not original. We're kind of bad at naming things. I once had a gerbil named Cornflakes." She paused. "Sorry, Daisy can be a little nervous around strangers."

Mr. Do's eyes brightened. He reached into a shirt pocket and pulled out a dog treat. "It's an old mail carrier's trick. Better to make friends than get bitten." He offered the treat with an open palm extended forward, but Daisy would not come near. The old man laughed, a mirthful, rolling chuckle. "No treat? There's a first time for everything!"

Willow furtively peered into the garbage bin. It was a snake after all. A dead snake about the width of a thin child's arm and twice as long. The old man noticed her gaze. He reached down and covered the snake with stray papers.

"Do you usually find snakes around here?" Ash asked. It was the first time he spoke. The man gave Ash a long look and shrugged. A non-answer.

Ash continued, "It just seems weird that—"

"I left a note on the desk in your room. I'll come back later to fix the faucet. Probably just need to replace a washer. This afternoon or tomorrow. We'll see. Will you be staying with us long?"

Daisy barked, twice, in protest of the idea.

"Another day, maybe two," Willow said. "My father hurt his neck."

"Hmm," Mr. Do said. "Some people, you'd be surprised. They stay a long, long time. Who knows why." He looked wistfully down the line of motel room doors. Each door represented a task to do. He bent to lift the ladder. Things to do, places to be. He smiled, gave the slightest bow, and began to move on.

"Did you happen to fix the vending machine?" Willow asked. "That monster ate my money."

Mr. Do raised a finger, eyes twinkling. "It works perfectly now. But be gentle with it. No banging, pushing, punching, kicking."

Ash gave Willow a soft push. "Of course. We only do that to each other."

Mr. Do scratched the back of his neck. As if the thought had just popped into his head. "A word to the wise. Stay out of the woods behind the motel. It's not safe."

"Why not?" Ash wondered aloud.

"Just—" Mr. Do said sharply. He caught himself, softened his tone. "The Whispering Pines are a part of a vast preserve. Behind us, there's town. But in that direction the wilderness goes back fifty miles. No roads, no rangers. The only trails are made by deer, moose, coyote, bear. Very easy to get turned around in there. It's happened before. A person could enter and become lost forever." He looked at Ash, raising a closed fist. "Poof," he said, opening his hand as if he'd just released a luminescent firefly. He looked up to the sky. "Gone forever. Just stay out of the woods."

A low rumble came from Daisy. She seemed to be working herself up to an actual growl. A rare thing for a goldendoodle. Mr. Do noticed. "Your dog doesn't care for me."

"Daisy's just nervous," Willow explained, soothing the dog with a gentle hand. "It's her first motel experience."

"Yes," Ash agreed. "She hasn't decided whether to trust you or not."

Mr. Do met Ash's comment with a curious stare. He finally smiled and opened his hands in a gesture of surrender. "A wise dog," the man said. "One must always be cautious in whom they place trust."

The children watched him go. Willow hugged Daisy, consoling the frightened dog. "Shh, shh," she said. "It was only mean old Mr. Do. You're safe with us."

"Hmm," Ash said.

"What?"

"I don't know, Will," he replied. "Something about that guy seems off."

"Daisy didn't like him, that's for sure," Willow said. "Did you get a look at that snake?"

Ash shook his head. "No, he covered it up too quickly. Why?"

"I can't swear to it," Willow said. "But I'm almost positive—it had *two heads*."

TWENTY

"I'M BRINGING YOUR FATHER into town for the MRI appointment," Mrs. McGinn announced. "It might take a while."

Willow and Ash shared hopeful sidelong glances.

Noticing this, their mother said, "On second thought, maybe I should insist on bringing you two along. It doesn't feel right to leave you here on your own."

"Mom," Willow protested. "Don't make us sit in a medical building all day. That's, like . . . cruel and unusual punishment. Besides, I'm thirteen. I've been babysitting for the past two years. If I can handle the evil Plankster twins, I can sit around here for a few hours, easy."

"We can take care of ourselves," Ash agreed. "Besides, I want to start reading that graphic novel you gave me about the Apollo missions. It looks really interesting."

It was a smart move, playing the book card. Mrs. McGinn was a school librarian. She would basically cut off her right arm if it would get her children to read. She checked the time on her phone. "Okay," she relented. "You two stick together—don't leave the grounds—and no quarreling. Understand? Call me if there's a problem."

Not knowing what the future held—or what dangers they would soon face—Willow and Ash made promises that they intended to keep. A small tremor shivered through their bodies. A few hours of freedom. No one to tell them what to do. A few minutes later, they waved goodbye, promised once more to behave, took the ten crisp singles their father had given them—and hit the vending machine, hard.

Ash took a moment to research *liminal space* on

Willow's phone. He quickly read through a few definitions. In architecture, it meant "the physical space between one destination and the next." An in-between place. On Wiki, it was described as "the 'crossing over' space—a space where you have left something behind, yet you are not fully in something else. A transition space."

"Come," Willow said.

Ash quickly thumbed the screen blank.

"I see that new girl," Willow said. "Let's go meet her."

Outside the fenced-in pool, there was a small pavilion with two picnic tables, a crumbling shuffleboard court, and the built-in grill where the McGinns had feasted the previous night. The girl who had arrived the previous day, Justice—Juss, for short—sat alone at one of the tables. She had a pad of drawing paper and a small plastic case with art supplies. Her crutches leaned precariously against the table.

"Hi," Willow said. "This is Ash, my brother. I'm Willow. Do you mind if we sit down with you?"

Justice's eyes twinkled, and she beamed a wide-open,

dimpled smile that shone like a lighthouse into a wine-dark sea. "Sure! Do you like to draw? I have extra paper if you want."

"I'm not very good," Willow admitted, accepting the offer. "Horses just about killed me. I couldn't draw a horse to save my life. They all ended up looking like sad dogs."

Justice laughed. "It takes practice. I like unicorns—a lot—too much, my dad says—he says I'm obsessive—so I'm actually pretty good." She talked quickly, the words pouring forth in a torrent. She opened her pad, hastily flipped through the pages, and held up a drawing of a unicorn in flight.

"Wow, you *are* good," Willow exclaimed. "I love the colors."

The three children drew quietly. Or not really. Willow and Ash were quiet—but Justice, they discovered, was an enthusiastic conversationalist. She talked *a lot*. But it was nice, hearing her voice, the gentleness of her thoughts. All the ideas in her head seemed to be battling it out to see which one could first escape from her mouth. After a short while, Justice's mother came out to scope out the situation, smiling when she saw the three kids all sitting together. She quickly disappeared, emerging a few minutes later with a big bowl of green grapes for everyone to share.

Willow and Justice drew imaginary fairy houses. Complete with fairies, of course. It was Justice's idea. Willow happily went along. She felt mellow and content. Drawing was fun and Willow had forgotten how much she enjoyed it.

Ash drew a white cat curled up beside a tree.

Daisy rested in the grass, her leash tied to the pool's iron fence. Justice shifted in her seat, and her crutches, which were leaned against the table, clanged to the ground.

"I'll get them," Willow said.

"I'm used to it," Justice said, shaking her head. "It only happens about fifteen times a day."

Willow swallowed. "Can I ask about your crutches?"

Justice set down her marker. She looked at Willow and made a decision. "I was born with a birth defect called spina bifida. Those crutches help me walk. That's about it."

"I'm sorry," Willow said. She glanced at Ash. "Do you mind that I asked?"

"No, I guess it's okay," Justice answered. "I mean, it would be nice to never have to talk about it. But it's way better than stares. I don't like it when people stare. That's so much worse."

"Your arms look super strong," Willow said. "Ash says my arms are like ramen noodles. Not so strong—but delicious!"

Justice laughed. She flexed her biceps and gave a sly head tilt. "Wonder Woman," she said, laughing.

After a minute, Justice changed the subject. She talked about art and her parents—her father wrote computer programs—and about getting stuck at the motel all day—how suddenly there was a problem with their car's exhaust manifold, whatever that meant, and they needed a replacement part or something. She listed her favorite television shows, in numerical order—and told them about her pet cat that had died a week ago—how she still cried about it—every night—and on and on.

Willow liked her very, very much.

Ash was very absorbed in his drawing. He'd

stopped listening. He had a lot on his mind. At the moment, he was pondering the mysterious Mr. Do. It was just a feeling, but he knew that man from somewhere, like they had met in a different dimension. The broken pool gate squeaked open. The sound of rust and disuse. It gave Ash an idea.

TWENTY-ONE

"GUYS, THIS IS SO COOL!" Ash exclaimed.

He was standing in the deep part of the empty pool. Cement walls towered above him on three sides, with the distant wall at the shallow end. He felt like a turtle in an echoing terrarium.

Willow and Juss came over. They looked down at him.

"I want to go down there," Juss said.

Willow looked at her. "Cool. Do you need help or—"

"Try and stop me," Juss answered.

It took some determined effort—step by step down

the stairs at the shallow end, then cautiously down the slippery incline into the deep end. Willow saw how Justice's knees could bend but not her ankles. Her feet were locked in place with plastic braces.

They were clearly in the company of an unstoppable chatterbox named Justice Brown.

"I've never been at the bottom of a pool before," Justice commented. "I'm glad it's not filled with water!" Her smile seemed to take up half her face, a girl who smiled with her whole heart and soul.

Willow and Ash brought down the art supplies and folding chairs. Justice's mother appeared at the edge, arms crossed. "Girl, seriously?" she said. "Do you really think this is a smart thing to do?"

"Kind of, yeah," Juss answered. "It's not like we're going to drown."

Her mother let out a deep sigh. But Ash could tell that there was pride mixed in it, too. If Juss was bound and determined to do something, then everybody might as well get out of the way. Juss's mother, Mrs. Brown, handed down a plastic pitcher of iced tea. "I'm going to take a quick shower," she said. "Your father's at the gas station, checking on the car. He has his interview later today; the station will loan him a rental if our car's not ready. Do you kids need anything before I disappear for a few minutes? A bathroom break or—"

"I'm good, Mama," Justice said. "Love you!"

And to Ash and Willow, Mrs. Brown asked, "Has my girl been talking your ears off? We call her the Motormouth at home."

Willow assured her that Justice was being awesome.

Everyone was happy except for Daisy, who was still leashed to the fence outside the pool. It was in her nature to be part of the pack. Alone, she was cut off and vulnerable. Goldendoodles are a mixed breed, part golden retriever, part poodle. Smush those two together and you get a golden-doodle. They became wildly popular for a few very good reasons. Goldendoodles, like poodles, don't shed, so there isn't dog hair all over the place. They are hypoallergenic—an especially important factor for anyone, such as Mr. McGinn, who is allergic to dogs. And lastly, best of all, they are supersweet and lovable. That was Daisy all right: a lover, not a fighter. In fact, Daisy was kind of a wimp. If big dogs scared her, small dogs scared her even worse. Thunder? Fireworks? Terrifying. She'd curl up into a ball, shivering in fright. Perhaps because of this, Daisy had one habit. She barked. Loud and often. The McGinns got used to it and learned to ignore the racket. And it slowly got better as Daisy, now almost seven, matured and felt more secure. But on nervous days, Daisy barked at anything. Passing cars and drifting clouds. At the wind, the rain, the leaves in the trees. *BarkbarkbarkyBARKbarkBARK!*

Oh well. Nobody's perfect. Not even dogs.

But to Willow and Ash, Daisy came close.

Today, for some reason, was a barking-at-everything day.

Willow finally announced, "I'm going to see about Daisy. Maybe get her some food from our parents' room—I might have to hunt around for the spare key. I'll see if she has enough water while I'm at it."

After a few minutes, Ash heard a new sound coming from Daisy. A whine and a high-pitched, startled *yip-yip.* Then the dog was silent.

"No more barking," Justice whispered to Ash, not taking her eyes off the page.

"Uh-huh," Ash replied.

The gate squeaked open again. Ash looked up expecting to see Willow. But he saw something else instead. Something large and ominous.

The dire wolf loped inside the pool area. Its dark gray tail was bushy and black-tipped. Its mottled fur was a combination of white, brown, gray, and black. Though huge with powerful haunches, the wolf looked lean, hungry for its next meal. Normally a wolf would steer far away from humans. But this one looked like it was stalking them.

The creature stood at the end of the wall nearest to them, peering down at Ash and Justice through intelligent eyes. Slivers of red flashed in them. An old scar zigzagged across its face. The wolf's upper lip lifted, exposing its sharp teeth. It snarled and locked eyes with Ash, who averted his gaze, not wishing to provoke it. Ash's every instinct told him to shrink, to lower, to make himself small. Maybe, even, invisible. Like last night. But he couldn't risk it—not with Justice here. Besides, some instinct told him that his camouflage trick wouldn't work on the wolf. The enormous, muscular wolf padded along the rim of the pool, pacing back and forth, restlessly planning its attack. Ash could smell a foul stench coming from its breath. He imagined dead prey, crushed bones, rancid meat.

It killed things to survive.

While the wolf tried to puzzle out a way to get at them—and it would soon realize that it could simply take the wide cement steps at the other end of the structure—Ash and Justice tried to figure out how to escape. No answers came to mind.

They were trapped.

And once again there was nowhere to hide.

TWENTY-TWO

A THOUGHT OCCURRED to Ash: *Maybe it's not real.* Maybe that enormous wolf up there, with sharp teeth and a powerful jaw, was just his imagination.

Nothing to worry about, nothing at all.

Isn't that what his parents had always said?

Just your imagination running away with you.

"Justice," he said in a soft voice. "Do you see it, too?"

Justice forced herself to look at the wolf. She nodded. Yes, she saw it all right.

Even in broad daylight, the wolf's eyes had a reddish tint. She crouched down and swiped a paw at

Ash. Her long, razor-sharp claws missed by only eighteen inches. Ash noticed tears shimmering in Justice's eyes. She chewed on her lower lip. Fingers fidgeting nervously. He reached for her hand and squeezed.

The wolf raised her snout and sniffed, picking up a scent. She moved toward the shallow end. Took one cautious step down the first stair. And another.

A long tongue licked hungry lips.

"She came for me," Ash whispered, moving his body protectively in front of the girl. "You'll be safe, Juss. Just be quiet. Try to stay calm. And if anything happens—look away."

"Nuh-uh," Justice retorted. "I'm not helpless. Papa taught me that. I know I can't run, and I can't hide— but I can think, and I can fight."

Justice picked up her crutches and held them high over her head, arms fully extended to the sky. *Clang,* she smashed the metal crutches together. The sharp, metallic crack startled the wolf. It was unpleasant in her large, rounded ears. *Clang, crash!* The sounds pierced the air like gunshots. Justice crashed the metal crutches together again, and again. The wolf looked agitated, suddenly uncertain. She paused, front paw dangling midstep.

Ash understood immediately. It wasn't time to shrink. It was time to grow. Time to be seen and heard. Ash took one of Justice's crutches. He stood tall and waved it over his head, trying to look as big and scary as possible. He roared, "AAAAHHHH!"

Justice joined in. "GET OUT OF HERE, WOLF! GO!" she shouted. "DON'T MESS WITH US!"

They waved the crutches wildly, at times crashing them together with a resounding clatter.

The wolf backed up the steps, turned away.

The great wolf swiveled her head, looking in the direction of the motel rooms. Some movement caught her eye. And in an instant, as if it never happened, the wolf moved like smoke through the open gate and was gone.

Justice and Ash sat waiting, unwilling to break the silence.

They were a movie put on pause. A screen capture.

"Is she gone?" Justice finally asked.

Ash heard the fear creep into Justice's voice. He saw that her eyes were on the brink of tears. He put his arm around her shoulders. "Yeah, I think so. Thanks to you."

Willow's voice called out from above. "Sorry I

TWENTY-THREE

WILLOW PICKED UP the dog collar, still attached to the leash tied to the fence. There was no sign of Daisy anywhere. Could she have gotten spooked by something? The dog had seemed so nervous lately.

Willow had been gone only ten minutes, tops. Mr. Do was underneath the sink, fixing the leaky faucet. He kept asking questions. It felt rude leaving him alone there. She had filled the water bowl and grabbed a handful of dog biscuits.

And now . . . no Daisy?

She felt a tightness in her chest, a fist of worry.

The road. Those big trucks hurtling past.

Ash called from the pool, "Help us up, Willow. We've got chairs and a lot of stuff here—and Juss is coming up, too. Are you sure you don't see Daisy? We need to find her."

Willow and Ash assisted Justice out of the pool, not that she couldn't do it herself. The slippery surface along the bottom was challenging. The crutches tended to slip, like walking on ice. So they were there for her. Willow at her side, Ash following close behind, just in case.

Before heading to her room, Justice turned to Ash. "So . . . that was intense, yeah?"

Ash nodded. "Yeah, if by *intense* you mean *terrifying*. You were really brave, Juss. Resourceful, too."

"Thanks," the younger girl replied.

"Are you going to tell your parents what happened?" Ash asked.

Willow looked at them curiously, her eyes asking, *What happened? Did it have anything to do with the disappearance of Daisy?*

"Are you kidding?" Justice replied, chin out, eyes wide. "They'd wrap me in Bubble Wrap and put me on a shelf. I'd never be allowed out again. I'm not saying a word."

"Ash," Willow said impatiently.

Ash nodded. "Yes, Daisy. I'll just get the chairs and—"

"Forget the chairs!" Willow snapped. "We need to find our dog, now."

"Go, you guys," Justice said. "I'll keep an eye out here."

"You sure?" Ash asked.

"I'm fine. Go," Justice insisted.

It made sense to first check the busy road. Daisy was oblivious enough to wander in front of traffic. Ash didn't think it was likely—but he didn't want to argue with his sister. It wasn't a debate he could win.

"Daisy, here girl, Daisy!" Willow shouted. There was no answer, no sign of her.

"The Whispering Pines," Ash said.

"You think?"

"She got spooked," Ash said. "The wolf came. I thought she was after me. But I think you might have scared her off."

"Why would Daisy go into the woods?" Willow wondered.

Ash shrugged. "I don't know—to hide, maybe? It doesn't matter. I'm almost certain that's where she went. I feel it in my bones."

They hurried to the same spot as before, where a bloodied Kristoff had emerged just yesterday morning.

Fear for Daisy, combined with a fierce desire to protect her, gave Ash and Willow the courage to plunge forward. They bent low and crawled on all fours through a tunnel of brambly, tangled under-growth. Soon the forest opened up and they were able to stand. Willow called for Daisy, listened, called again. The trees were tall, allowing enough space for sunlight to filter through. Dry pine needles carpeted the ground.

Willow pointed out a well-established deer trail. "This way, you think?"

"I do," Ash answered.

Surrounded by forest, beneath the shade of mostly spruces and pines, Ash felt a peculiar sensa-tion. A tingling in his nerve endings. He looked up at the towering trees, reaching to the light. But then his thoughts were drawn downward to the earth's soil. He could feel how each tree was connected underground—a network of overlapping roots.

Communicating with one another.

One forest, one tree, one mind.

It was all connected.

And he felt connected . . . to it.

Ashhhhh, the murmurings began. *Yessss, thissss way.*

Was it just the rustling of leaves? The swishing of the wind? Or was Ash somehow connected to the network of roots beneath his feet? The boy glanced at his sister. Did Willow hear it, too? No, she showed no sign of it. The voices were for him alone. Ash and Willow kept following the path, pausing to shout Daisy's name, waiting, hoping, pushing on.

Willow became frustrated. "I don't know, Ash. What if Daisy went back to the room?"

"Justice said she'd keep an eye out," he reasoned. "This is the way. Trust me."

"How do you know?"

He stopped to look at her. Willow was scared.

Not for herself but for their dog. For Daisy. "We'll find her," he said in what he hoped was a confident voice.

They kept walking.

Closssser, getting clossser, the voices whispered, impossible sounds brushing the hushes.

The trail narrowed and became less certain. Vines twisted on the ground and wrapped around tree trunks. The canopy grew thicker, letting in less light. The air felt thick, stuffy, hard to breathe.

Sssstray not, the voices warned. Each voice overlapping, intermingling, one voice coming from different sources. The trees speaking one thought. Ash stopped, dropped to his knees, felt the ground with his fingertips, listened.

"Ash, what—"

"Shhhh," he said. Ash bent his head lower, closer to the earth. He strained to hear the rumblings of the root system, the network of chemical pulses.

The trees breathed. They lived. They spoke.

Dangerssss lurk . . . sssstray not from the path, Ashhhhh.

Willow's hand gripped his shoulder. "LB," she said softly. There was anxiety in her voice. "There's something behind those trees . . . shadows moving."

It was difficult to see any distance. Ash squinted, closed his eyes, opened them again. A shape, a blur, moved behind the trees. He turned to the right and shivered. A clammy draft came over him, brushed against his side. His heart pounded, swollen in his chest. Some creatures were out there. Bad, bad things. Stalking them, watching.

Creatures they *almost* saw.

Willow took photos, randomly aiming into the shadows.

"We can't stay here," Ash urged. "Come on. Whatever you do, don't stray from the path."

Getting closssser, the voices called.

"We're getting closer," he told his sister.

Willow looked at him, confused. *How does he know?*

"DAISY!" she screamed. "Daisy, come!"

After a long, empty silence, a mournful cry threaded through the forest. Daisy's sorrowful whine.

"That's her!" Willow enthused. She pushed past Ash and raced up the path. The ground inclined beneath their feet. They were moving steeply uphill,

TWENTY-FOUR

NOT A TREE, not a bush, not a flower or a weed.

Willow and Ash had stepped into a barren, unearthly clearing. A perfect circle on a flat hilltop about fifty feet across in all directions. An unnatural place. Nothing grew there. Nothing lived there. Except for the tangled vines that were coiled around Daisy's torso, head, and legs, pinning the dog to the ground. Daisy looked helplessly toward her owners. Like a fly trapped in a spiderweb, Daisy was unable to move any part of her body. Trapped, the dog gave a sad, desperate, frightened whine.

It was a heartbreaking sight. Willow and Ash

hurried to their dog, working feverishly to free Daisy from the tightening vines. Willow worked near Daisy's head, making reassuring noises of love and affection. "We got you, girl, we got you."

Ash started on her legs. The vines seemed to resist his efforts. He unwound a section, only to watch in amazement as they curled back in place. He searched the area and found two sharp-edged rocks. He handed one to Willow. "Cut it with this. Watch, see what I'm doing?" He slashed away at the vines, tearing off pieces and throwing them away.

After an agonizing ten minutes, Daisy was free.

She stood . . . and collapsed. "Daisy's too weak to walk," Willow said.

Movement in his periphery caused Ash to turn his head. A piece of discarded vine wriggled on the ground. Like a snake, it writhed and slithered in their direction. "We gotta go, Will." He scooped up Daisy in his arms. "We gotta go now!"

They ran, stumbling, blundering forward, panicked. Ash ripped up his legs when a prickly bush appeared in his path. Willow tripped over a root and fell heavily, tearing skin from her hands. Her foot became ensnared by the forest growth. She yanked it free, cursing and kicking.

Brother and sister ran until they could run no more. Daisy weighed thirty-five pounds—but she felt so much heavier. Willow, who was stronger, older, and more athletic than Ash, took a long turn carrying Daisy. They finally slowed to a walk. Paused to rest. Panting in the forbidden forest.

Daisy sniffed and let out a growl.

A presence stalked them in the shadows.

A layer of fog rolled along the ground, covering their feet and ankles.

Ash saw eyes in the mist.

AWOOOOOO!

Willow and Ash felt their hearts seize up, like an engine that suddenly stalled. Daisy stood on her own and took a few tentative steps. Fear gave her strength. "That's good, Daisy," Willow said, encouraged. "Let's go. Come on, you can do it."

And in that way—panting, frightened, haunted, and hunted by unseen creatures—they made their way out of the Whispering Pines.

Glad to be alive.

They sprawled on the grass, breathing hard. Daisy curled into a tight ball, pressed close against Willow's side.

A voice reached Ash's ears.

Ashhhhh, there are otherssss.

Otherssss to resssscue.

And ever so faintly, a distant yowling came to him. A small forgotten cat—lost and alone—mewling for help.

Ash didn't try to answer.

He didn't say a word.

Not to the trees, or the breeze or the leaves, and especially not to Willow. This was a secret he would keep to himself. *Was it all a dream? Another fantasy? Was any of this real?* It didn't matter anymore.

They got Daisy back.

Safe and sound.

But another thought pulled on his sleeve for attention.

There are others.

In that moment, Ash didn't know if it was *his thought* at all—or if instead the idea had come to him, drifting eerily in the wind, from some hidden realm in the Whispering Pines.

Others to rescue?

What did it even mean?

What did the forest mind want from him?

TWENTY-FIVE

MR. MCGINN'S MRI took forever but came back "clean," as the doctors described it. He simply needed to take it easy, rest up, and not try to do too much.

"So he's going to live?" Willow wisecracked.

"Looks like it," Mrs. McGinn said. "We'll leave tomorrow morning, bright and early."

"Not too early, I hope," Ash said. He preferred to sleep late when given the chance.

They were gathered in their parents' attached room, which had a small eating nook by the front window with two chairs. The door that separated rooms 15 and 16 was now open, connecting all four family members and Daisy, too.

Mrs. McGinn took out a prescription bottle. She opened it—expertly pressing down the cap and turning—and pulled out one pill. She shook the pills that remained in the bottle. "You won't be needing all these. It's crazy that doctors write prescriptions for so many pills. A person could get addicted. I'm throwing them away."

"Just one for tonight and that's it?" their father asked, a little wistfully. He had already discarded the neck brace. But giving up the pain pills made him nervous.

"Yes," she said. "You'll sleep deeply tonight. After that, it's Advil and Tylenol. No more addictive pain-killers for my wonderful husband."

Without discussing it, Ash and Willow took turns comforting Daisy. They snuggled close and kept her in sight. They sensed that what Daisy needed most of all was love and cuddles. The siblings were more than happy to provide both.

While Ash kept close to Daisy indoors, Willow wandered outside for fresh air. She needed time to think, or "process," as she liked to say. She sat on a stone bench in the rock garden. There was a gravel path with neat, hand-printed identifications for the different wildflowers. Once again, it struck Willow as somewhat odd: The garden was meticulously cared for while the motel itself was in a state of neglect. The garden was someone's labor of love— and she doubted that someone was named Kristoff. He didn't seem like the wildflower type.

Wi-Fi was erratic at the motel. There were hot spots and dead zones constantly swapping places. Willow had all but given up on getting the internet. She pulled out her phone, eager to review the photos from the Pines. The shots were uniformly dark, except for those taken in the treeless hilltop clearing. In her panic, Willow neglected to take any photos of Daisy. No matter. She could still see it in her imagination, knew that she would see it forever burned into her memory. Daisy trapped, helpless, tied down, tangled in vines.

How could such a thing happen?

Who—or what—could have done it?

She applied a variety of edit features to the photos,

lightening, highlighting, sharpening the images. Nothing came forward. If there were living creatures hiding in the woods, they didn't appear in her photographs. There was no sign of Ash's dire wolf. Willow set the phone aside, open to a dull, featureless photo taken of the surrounding forest. She looked to the sky. The late-afternoon sun was hidden by dark clouds. Willow wondered if it might rain.

She glanced down and stared in disbelief. The picture on the phone showed upward from its place on the bench. Willow blinked. She shook her head. What on earth was going on? She took a closer look at the photo. It was impossible. She was absolutely sure of that. *The photo had changed.* In the middle of the same picture that before had showed only the edge of the clearing and the woods now walked a cat. A small, undernourished white cat. It was walking directly to the camera, no more than ten feet from Willow when she had snapped the photo.

She had seen no cat.

There was no cat in the picture a few minutes ago. Of that, Willow was certain. But there was now. A cute cat with one bent ear. It was injured. One eye was almost shut, scratched and swollen. A thin trail of yellow pus leaked from it. No matter how Willow held the phone—up, down, to the side—the cat's good eye stared directly at her. Willow stood, her body quivering. This was crazy. It was too much. There had to be some kind of explanation. Nothing made sense since the minute they had arrived here. Willow noticed Kristoff standing outside the office. He turned and went back inside. It was time to get some answers. No one was in the office when she opened the door. As she reached for the bell on the counter, the sound of a raised voice paused her hand. It was Kristoff, just on the other side of the door to his private residence. And he seemed stressed.

"Mom, you have to be more careful. If someone sees you, we're finished. I can't argue now, Mom. Just don't go anywhere, please. You aren't acting like yourself. Please, I'm begging you. This has to stop." The doorknob turned, and Willow quickly slammed her hand down on the bell, *DING!*

Kristoff opened the door.

"Wow, that was fast!" Willow exclaimed.

Kristoff eyed her closely. He cocked his head. "Have you been listening?"

"What? *Pffft*," Willow replied unconvincingly. She shrugged. "I mean, I heard you talking to someone."

"My mother," Kristoff said.

"Were you fighting? You sounded upset."

Kristoff absently tapped the wolf ring on the counter. "No, I wouldn't say that."

"We're leaving tomorrow," Willow announced. "We never expected to stay three nights in the first place."

"Yes, your father informed me. I'm glad he's feeling better." *Tap-tap.* The ring tapped against the counter again. "But, Willow"—he said, looking away—"I'll be sorry to see you go."

That surprised her. A show of warmth. Even affection, maybe. He was usually cold and distant. For that one second, he let down his guard.

"It must be hard—watching people come and go," Willow observed.

"We get some repeat visitors," Kristoff countered. "But, yes, you're right. This is a place where people, like yourself, come and go. I don't make any lasting friends. I wish you could hang around longer."

Willow stepped close to the counter. She looked directly into his dark eyes. "Can you be honest with me, please?"

Kristoff exhaled. He nodded once, wordlessly.

"We went into the woods," Willow said.

"I warned you to stay—"

"Yeah, but we didn't, okay," Willow rejoined. "My dog was lost and that's all I cared about. If you had a pet, you'd understand."

Kristoff pursed his lips. He understood.

"What is the actual deal with those woods?" Willow asked. "Ash and I saw some strange things. Daisy was tied up in vines."

"Your dog? Is she okay?" Kristoff asked. He seemed genuinely concerned.

"Yes," Willow answered. "A little freaked out—but safe. Answer my question. What's the deal?"

Kristoff sank into his chair. His thumb pressed against a front tooth. "There are all sorts of legends and tall tales and falsehoods. People say that those woods are full of ghosts. They say it's a magical place.

Some locals tell stories about swampland—about travelers who entered and never returned."

"I think there are animals in there."

"Well, sure," Kristoff said. "Every forest is going to have wildlife. Why, just this morning I watched as a doe and her fawn nibbled on our hostas right outside that window."

"I'm not talking about Bambi," Willow snapped.

Kristoff swallowed. "Okay, okay." He took a deep breath, tapped the ring on the counter as a method of focusing his thoughts. *Tap-tap-tap.* "The ghosts that people claim to have seen—and you are not the first—are always *animals.*"

"I'm listening," Willow said.

"There's something wrong in those woods," Kristoff said. "A poison or—I couldn't guess. A virus, perhaps. A strain of rabies."

"Ash said the rabbits were scary somehow." Willow rolled her eyes, acting as if she were not entirely convinced of her brother's story. "You know how it is— killer bunnies, big teeth." She curled two fingers in front of her mouth for a comical killer-bunny effect.

Kristoff smiled thinly.

"Willow, please. You must stay away from any animals you encounter. Any animal with rabies can be dangerous."

Willow nodded, smiled, and thanked Kristoff for his honesty. It was all very helpful. But inside she knew that he was only telling half-truths and lies. There were secrets that he was still unwilling to surrender. Oh well. They were running out of time. Leaving tomorrow. Not every mystery gets solved.

"Some of the animals"—Kristoff volunteered—"seem a little dead."

"Dead?"

"Muted, lacking spark. It's the virus, I think," Kristoff ventured. "It's like they went into those woods . . . and came back . . . but were never the same. Something changed inside them. They were broken in some way, as if a part of those animals never returned."

"And Daisy?" Willow asked.

Kristoff's lips tightened into a thin line. "I hope that you saved her in time."

TWENTY-SIX

EARLIER THAT DAY, Ash had *borrowed* the flashlight from his parents' bag. *Borrowed* was such a better word than *stole*. Now Willow was asleep in bed. *How many thirteen-year-old girls snore?* he wondered. On bare feet, he listened by the door that adjoined the two rooms. The television played at a low volume. That's how his parents often fell asleep, hypnotized by satellites bouncing signals through the atmosphere. Technology was a trip. And TV put everybody to sleep.

Grabbing his sneakers, Ash silently slipped out into the night. He'd been given a mission.

There were others.

Others to be rescued.

Ash picked his way around the building and came to a jarring stop. Justice stood at the vending machine, chewing thoughtfully, a half-eaten Snickers bar in her fist. "Shhhh," she said. "I'm sneaking this."

"Whew, you startled me," Ash said, his hand on his chest. "I must be getting jumpy. But yeah, Snickers—good call. I came to grab something, too."

"We're leaving tomorrow," Justice said. "My dad had an interview for a job." She shrugged. "He thinks he might get it. We spent half the day looking at houses."

"That's awesome," Ash said.

Justice stood watching him. She pointed to the vending machine. "Are you going to—"

"Oh right, yeah," Ash said. He patted his pockets, front and back. "I'm such a space cadet. I forgot my money."

Justice gave him a look. "I know where you are going. I'd come with you if I could."

"I have to go alone," he confessed.

"I know," she said. "The wolf."

"Please don't tell."

Justice paused. She did not, for once, smile. "I won't lie for you."

"That's disappointing," Ash said. "Justice, I was wondering. Do you hear them, too. The voices?"

"I saw that big bad wolf with the scar across her face," Justice answered. "Do you know anyone else who saw it?"

Ash thought back. It hadn't occurred to him before.

"You're not the only one with a gift," she said, before swinging past him and turning the corner without so much as a glance over her shoulder. She wouldn't have seen him, anyway. Ash was already gone, flashlight on, blazing a sword of light into the darkness.

It rained that night. A slashing rain that poured down slantways. At first, the canopy of trees protected him like an umbrella. But not for long. The branches dampened and dripped. Gusts of wind shook the trees, shaking the water off. Ash walked steadily on. Not fully conscious but almost trancelike. A sleepwalker tuned to a strange frequency. Ash's entire sensory system became a tuning fork. His body and brain hummed to the mysterious language of the ancient forest.

There are otherssss . . . otherssss to be ssssaved.

Mud appeared in low depressions. His sneakers squelched in standing water. Tree roots became slick and treacherous. The dead branch of a tree clawed at his arm. Rain streamed from his hair down his cheeks. Wind tore through the leaves. Trees crashed and fell to the ground. Some were caught in the arms of another. The ground became littered with debris and deadfall. And still Ash walked on, following the flashlight's hazy, milky light.

Then he stopped—stopped cold—and seemed to open his eyes for the first time. The spell had lifted. He was fully awake, returned to the open clearing. What had come over him? He barely remembered walking through the woods—or up the hill—or why he'd even come.

The rain slowed and, then, suddenly stopped. The waxing moon broke free from the clouds. The clearing shone under its ghostly light. It looked false somehow. Ash had scratches on his arm. He was wet and dirty. Beyond the clearing, he sensed the vast, unlit, sprawling wilderness. Shadow upon shadow. Everything was still and silent. A warmth seeped into his body. He shivered. An icy finger of fear ran down his spine.

He kept walking. He had come too far to stop now.

The ground tilted. He found himself moving down beyond the other side of the clearing, deeper into the woods.

Dead tree limbs looked like old bones picked clean and tossed away, toothpicks for a giant.

Careful, a voice whispered.

Or we all fall down.

Ash hesitated, as if standing at the edge of the world. He sensed a narrow path in the darkness. And a creature waiting there for him. The flashlight could scarcely penetrate into the thick copse of twisting, turning oaks.

The boy turned off the light. It was useless anyway. He left the clearing and crossed over.

TWENTY-SEVEN

WILLOW HAD HEARD HIM GO. The door clicked, and she opened her eyes.

She instantly knew where he was going.

And why he went alone.

Her brave, troubled little brother.

Listening to voices in his head.

Still she felt paralyzed, unable to move. She lay in bed, ears pricked to the pitch of night. Faint voices. The sound of Justice and her crutches, swinging her legs together as one. Willow leaped up and opened the door.

"Did you see him?" Willow asked.

Justice frowned, nodded reluctantly, yes.

"Did he go—"

"Into the woods," Justice interrupted.

"I have to follow him."

"I know," Justice said. "Everyone has a part to play."

The wind began to stir. Dust and dirt swirled from the parking lot. "What else do you know?" Willow asked.

Justice avoided the question. "It's going to rain. You'll need a flashlight."

Willow didn't have a raincoat, but she pulled on a hoodie, socks, and sturdy sneakers. She planned on using her phone as a flashlight. Hopefully the battery would last. There was no choice. She had to go.

Daisy scratched at the door.

"You want to come?" Willow asked, surprised.

The dog pawed at the carpet, nosed against the door, and gave out an urgent cry. Willow considered the leash for a long moment. Something told her no. They stepped out together.

All his life, Ash had been different. Special in ways no one could explain. He was *sensitive* to things. Felt more deeply than other people. He sensed things and, Willow had long suspected, saw things, too. *Invisible things.* And now he was hearing voices. For a long time, she was amused by it—LB, her nutty brother—then she became baffled, confused, and finally concerned. He complained about headaches. Pressure behind his eyes. Why hadn't she listened?

Willow paused, glancing all around. It was all but impossible to see. She walked onward. *Crack*, a heavy tree branch fell with a heavy thud in the space Willow had just occupied. A moment sooner and she would have been crushed. Killed in the woods in the dark of night. More branches. The dangers escalated. Willow slipped and ripped her pants at the knee, the phone skittering from her hand. Willow picked it up. The light shone on a muddy footprint. Her heart leaped. The rain kept falling. She hurried after her brother.

Daisy raced up ahead, nose to the ground. Willow followed. She walked and walked, calling after her brave dog. Daisy circled back, hurried forward, as if beseeching Willow to hurry. Finally they came to a dead end. The path . . . just . . . vanished.

WHAT ARE YOU DOING OUT HERE?

YOU ARE SHIVERING.

SO COLD.

Willow turned in a slow circle. Nothing looked familiar. Every tree, every bush—it all looked the same. The light from her phone flickered. "No, no, no." Willow groaned, shaking the phone. She checked the charge. Watched it drop from 2 percent to 1 percent to full dark.

"Ash!" she cried. "ASH!"

No answer.

In the distance, a wolf howled.

Somewhere closer, another answered.

Daisy leaned hard against Willow's legs. The dog gazed up at her human. "Okay, girl," Willow said, bending to hold the dog's head with two hands. "I'll follow you. No more dead ends, okay?"

The dog led her through the night maze of trees and undergrowth. Willow tripped, slipped, banged her head against low-hanging branches. She began to feel hopeless. Turned around. Following a dog! What an idiot! Something caught her eye. A faint light floating through the woods, appearing and disappearing as it passed behind trees and boulders.

Ash? she wondered.

In answer, Daisy took off like a shot, crashing through the pathless woods.

Ash heard muffled noises in the distance. Rustling. The breaking of sticks, the sound of an animal moving swiftly toward him. He crouched defensively, scanning into the darkness with the beam of his flashlight. *Wait . . . could it be?*

"Whoa, Daisy! You scared me. What are you doing here?" Ash paused, piecing the puzzle together. "WILL?" he called. "WILLOW MCGINN? CAN YOU HEAR ME??!!"

Daisy raced off again—thrilled to play this game—now in the direction of Willow. Ash carved a path in pursuit, fortunate to still have a functioning flashlight.

"I was lost—and wet—and my phone died," Willow stammered, her emotions raw from the strain of holding it together. Ash leaned in awkwardly to hug her, turning his body to the side.

"I've got something," he said. It was in the crook of his right arm, cradled close to his chest.

Ash shone the flashlight for Willow to see.

"Ah," Willow said. "Well, hello there, kitty!"

Daisy pushed in for a sniff, opened her mouth, and gave the little cat a big, wet, slurpy lick.

TWENTY-EIGHT

BACK IN THE ROOM, Willow attended to the needs of their new visitor. She gently toweled him off and offered him Daisy's food and water. "I wish we had milk," Willow commented.

"Tomorrow," Ash counseled.

Willow sat on her heels on the floor, transfixed by the new arrival. Daisy rested on a blanket but with both eyes wide open. "We should name him," Willow said.

"You know we can't keep it, Will. Dad's allergies."

Willow hadn't forgotten about her sneezy father.

How could she? It was the reason why all her requests for pets had been denied—until hypoallergenic Daisy came along. She'd heard that hairless cats didn't bother allergy sufferers. She'd seen pictures, tried to imagine loving one, but she couldn't quite get there.

A little gross if you asked Willow.

Ash was exhausted. He washed up in the bathroom but didn't want to run the shower with his parents in the next room. They'd know something was up. A few minutes later, he was zonked out in bed, one arm hanging to the floor.

Willow continued her examination of the cat. It was . . . different. First, physically, the little cat was underfed. No meat to it at all. Light as a feather. Remarkable he had survived. One ear was slightly bent, which was adorable. "It gives you character," she told the cat. But that other eye. It was clouded and swollen. Willow doubted he could even see out of it. Willow gently dabbed away the yellowish pus that drained from it.

But it wasn't that. There was something in the cat's manner that seemed . . . what was the word?

Remote. Here but not here. The cat walked stiffly away from Willow to curl up, instead, next to Daisy. Willow yawned, looked up at her bed. It seemed so far away. So she pulled down a blanket, reached up for a pillow, and slept on the floor beside Daisy and . . . the unnamed, one-eyed, slightly smelly rescue cat.

The next morning, gathered in their parents' room, they had to do some fast talking. Mr. McGinn even seemed a little defeated about it. "We've been through this, guys. The allergies make my eyes itch. I just can't."

"We know, honest, Dad, it's okay," Ash said. "We didn't even want a cat, really. It's just that this one—"

"We heard it crying," Willow piped up. "It was raining so hard. Out in the parking lot! I just had to take it in."

Mr. McGinn glanced at his wife, seeking an ally. He squeezed his nose between his thumb and the crook of his index finger. Sniffled. Their kind-hearted father hated to deprive his children of anything. His wife was much tougher minded.

"What's the plan now?" he wondered. "I mean, we're supposed to check out of here in a couple of hours. We can't just leave it by the side of the road."

The cat had lapped up some milk. Mrs. McGinn had driven to the twenty-four-hour convenience center to buy a bag of dry cat food and a can of salmon. Even so, the cat wasn't particularly affectionate. It kept a cool distance.

"It doesn't purr," Ash noted out of the blue.

All eyes turned to the cat sitting on the floor swishing its tail.

"I don't like it," Mrs. McGinn said.

"Mom!" Willow exclaimed.

"I'm not going to lie to you, honey," Mrs. McGinn said. She was brushing on eyeliner in front of the mirror. "I'm not a cat person, you know that. And this one . . . I'm not feeling it."

The cat arched its back and hissed.

It swiped at the air.

"Okay, that's odd," Mrs. McGinn said. "So what's the plan, kiddies? You took in a stray. It doesn't trust people. It might even have diseases. Now you have to deal with it."

"What about Kristoff?" Willow turned to Ash. "He could keep it as the motel cat. How hard could it be?"

"It needs love," Ash said. He picked up the young cat. It held itself stiffly in his arms, longing to escape. "Shhhh, shhhh," he said. "Actually, I have another idea. Come on, Will."

They found Justice sitting on a blue chair outside room 9. Her father, a wiry man with a full beard and mustache, loaded luggage into the trunk of their car. He didn't pay them any mind.

"Oh, look at that sweetie!" Justice gushed. "Can I hold it?"

"He's a little—I don't know—maybe not used to people," Ash said.

Justice waved the comment away. "Don't be ridiculous."

The cat allowed itself to be placed in Justice's arms. The girl paused and looked up at Ash. "Where did you find it?"

Ash tilted his head in the direction of the woods. "You know, around."

"His poor eye!" Justice exclaimed. "He needs to

see a vet. Dad! This cat needs to get to a vet!"

Mr. Brown paused long enough to look over his shoulder. "What's that you got there, baby?"

"This sad, homeless, beautiful cat," Justice said. "I love it!"

"You can keep it if you want," Willow offered.

"Dad?"

Mr. Brown shook his head. Waved his hands. "Talk to your mother, Juss. You know that's not my department." He stood upright—a tall man, at least six foot three inches—and took a long look at his daughter. If the animal had resisted the boy, it sank easily into Justice's arms.

After a brief discussion with Mrs. Brown, it was decided.

Justice had adopted a new pet.

An animal that was rescued out of the Whispering Pines. Not that anyone else needed to know the details about that. How Ash had crossed over, into the beyond, and carried it back.

"Oh, its tongue is cold," Justice said.

"Yeah, it's probably been a stray for a while," Willow speculated. "The left ear looks chewed up.

I don't think it can see out of that bad eye."

"Shut up, Will," Ash scolded. "We're trying to find this cat a new home."

Justice laughed, the joyful laugh that always came out like a shout. "It's mine now; you're not getting it back. This little guy looks perfect to me—all it needs is some good food, a good home, and lots of good lovin'."

TWENTY-NINE

IT WAS TIME TO LEAVE. Mr. McGinn was energized, bouncing around on the balls of his feet, talking about the sights they'd see, the places they would go. For a moment there, Willow felt a pang of pure horror when her father almost leaned in to hug Kristoff goodbye. The hotel clerk, Willow's vampire hottie, had stepped outside to wash the front windows. He had a blue spray bottle and a roll of paper towels tucked under his arm. As the family climbed into the car, Kristoff stared for an extra beat at Willow. He raised a hand and gave a passing smile. Without thinking, she blew him a kiss and laughed.

"Ooooooh," Ash teased.

"I can't believe I did that. I'm such a dork." Willow groaned.

"It's okay—you'll never see him again," Ash said.

Willow pulled the headphones over her ears.

Ash heard her sigh.

"Be sure to come back someday," Kristoff called, sending them off.

Mr. McGinn put the car in reverse, half turned to look out the rear window, and muttered under his breath, "Not likely."

"Dad, you never know," Willow protested. "We might come back someday."

"Oh, we know." Mrs. McGinn laughed. "Take a good look, kids. We are *not* going to spend another night in this dump. I can't believe you liked it. *There was no water . . . in the . . . pool!*"

Ash felt a tide of uneasiness sweep over him. A sense of—it was hard to say—gravity's tug. The way it calls a leaf to the ground. He felt that same pull coming from the motel. Behind the building, the impressive trees kept their vigil. Ash knew there were secrets hidden in the Whispering Pines. He had glimpsed a shadow of a greater mystery during his time in the beyond. When he had crossed over and came back. Secrets that now he'd never learn.

There were others still to save.

Things left undone.

Rooms left unexplored.

Oh well. At least they had managed to rescue Train, the nervous cat that Justice adopted. The thought of it made him smile. Heading down the driveway, he took one final look back. Mr. Do was in the rock garden wearing a wide-brimmed straw hat. He bent to pick a weed. To the left, over his shoulder, Kristoff pulled the trigger of the spray bottle. He wiped the office window in a circular motion.

Willow reached across Daisy to find Ash's hand. She squeezed it briefly, sadly. Another secret. Her fragile heart. In a funny way, neither sibling wanted to leave. "In a weird way, I liked it there," Willow said softly, as much to herself as to anyone. Ash knew how she felt. Sometimes it's hard to say goodbye. He felt the pull of the place.

The drive, like all long drives, was a blur. The kids

checked out. Snoozed, listened to music, sat stupefied. Ash tried to read, but it was hard to do in the car and made him feel vaguely nauseous. He heard his parents discussing the directions. It felt tense up there. His mother got like that when they made a wrong turn.

"It shouldn't be taking this long," she said.

"Now, now, dear," Mr. McGinn said. "We just got a little turned around, that's all."

They passed a familiar convenience store.

Turned right . . . drove up a winding driveway . . . and pulled into the parking lot of Exit 13 Motel.

Ash looked out the car window.

Kristoff sprayed the office window, wiping it in a circular motion.

In the garden, Mr. Do bent to pick a weed.

The world glitched.

"Dad? Mom?" Willow said. "What are we doing back here?"

Mr. McGinn shook his head, rubbed his eyes. "I don't—"

He didn't bother to finish the sentence.

Just turned around and headed out again.

"We must need gas," Mrs. McGinn said. "I filled it

up this morning, but we've been driving for hours."

"Gas gauge must be broken," Mr. McGinn groaned. "The needle is pointing at full. That's great, another thing broken."

They stopped to refuel, just to be safe. The tank was filled to the top after adding less than half a gallon. Mr. McGinn looked at the convenience store. "I'm going inside, see if I can get directions," he said.

He pulled on the front doors of the store. They were locked.

He leaned against the window, using his hands to block the sun from his eyes. There was no one inside. Not a soul.

He rapped a fist against it. "Hello? Hello?" he cried. "Anybody in there?"

Strange.

They managed to get back on the highway. Gave a hopeful cheer.

And drove, and drove.

"We got lucky," their mother said. "There's no traffic."

"There's no cars . . . at all," their father observed.

They drove in silence. A mounting feeling of tension, like a tightening knot, began to infect the atmosphere. There was no chatter. No bickering. Nothing at all. Just a collective feeling of anxiety and dread, drowning in silence.

"Look," Ash said. "The sign."

EXIT 13 MOTEL

"STOP BY FOR SOME SHUT-EYE!"

TAKE THE NEXT RIGHT IN 1.5 MILES.

ALL PETS WELCOME!

"That's impossible," Mr. McGinn said. He turned to his wife. "You're my copilot. What's going on? How could we be here again?"

They blew past the exit and kept driving on the empty road.

"Isn't it weird?" Willow asked. "All this time without seeing any cars?"

"Are you hungry, kids?" Mrs. McGinn asked, hoping to change the subject. Because yes, obviously it was weird. It was very weird.

And a little terrifying.

No one was hungry. All this time in the car, but they felt just as full as after they had chowed down breakfast sandwiches at the motel. Daisy wasn't restless at all. Didn't whine, or change positions, or need to pee. She just slept, curled in a ball, calm as a cucumber.

They passed the sign again.

"Now that makes no sense," Mr. McGinn complained. He slapped the steering wheel in frustration.

"Make the turn," Mrs. McGinn said. "I need to see this with my own eyes."

They drove up the winding driveway . . . and pulled into the parking lot of Exit 13 Motel.

Kristoff sprayed the same window, wiping it in a circular motion.

In the garden, Mr. Do bent to pick a weed.

"Dad? Mom?" Willow said. "What are we doing back here?"

Mr. McGinn shook his head, rubbed his eyes. "I don't—"

He stared at his wife, open-mouthed.

Again they turned around. Passed the same

convenience station. Got back on the empty highway. Drove and drove.

"Look," Ash said. "The sign."

EXIT 13 MOTEL

"STOP BY FOR SOME SHUT-EYE!"

TAKE THE NEXT RIGHT IN 1.5 MILES.

ALL PETS WELCOME!

This time when the car pulled into the lot, they all exited the car.

Boom, the driver's door slammed shut.

Kristoff turned away from wiping the window.

Mr. Do stood watching them, a weed in his hand.

"Back so soon?" Kristoff called. "What did you forget?"

"'So soon'?" Mr. McGinn repeated in astonishment. "We've been driving for hours."

Kristoff laughed. He looked up at the sun. It hadn't moved from its place in the sky. "You just left!"

Both parents went to talk privately with Kristoff.

Ash and Willow walked in the opposite direction

with Daisy. They went to the garden. Mr. Do's eyes squinted in the sun. "Pulling weeds, pulling weeds," he mumbled. "All I ever do is pull weeds . . . here at Exit 13 Motel."

"Kids! Come on, let's go. Get in the car!" Mr. McGinn shouted.

"Deckland, are you sure?" his wife said, sounding the first, faint note of protest.

"No, no, no," he snapped back. And harsher this time. Getting meaner and more frustrated. "Willow, Ash. NOW!"

No one seems to know who said it first. Some people credit Benjamin Franklin. Others claim that it was Albert Einstein. And it doesn't really matter because the quote is still a good one: "The definition of insanity is doing the same thing over and over again and expecting different results."

The McGinns set out in the car, again and again, to test that theory.

Finally, with a deep sigh, they pulled back up the long, winding driveway.

Ash looked out from the car.

The sun hung in its same place in the sky.

Kristoff sprayed the office window, wiping it in a circular motion.

In the garden, Mr. Do bent to pick a weed.

"Dad? Mom?" Willow said. "What are we doing back here?"

Mr. McGinn shook his head, rubbed his eyes.

He reached for his wife's hand. He said, "I love you, honey. No matter what happens."

Kristoff walked over to the car.

He handed over two sets of key cards for rooms 15 and 16.

"We've been expecting you," he said.

ABOUT THE AUTHOR

JAMES PRELLER is the author of many books for young children, including the popular Jigsaw Jones series and his middle-grade novels *Along Came Spider* and *Justin Fisher Declares War!* He lives in Delmar, New York, with his wife, Lisa; three children—Nicholas, Maggie, and Gavin; two cats; and a goldendoodle named Daisy.